The Executioner was a micro-second behind the bomber

The terrorist squeezed the trigger, and Bolan heard the hammer fall on an empty pistol.

Wasting no time, he sent a trio of rounds into the man's face, knocking him against the shattered stained-glass windows like a spineless rag doll.

All the terrorists at the back of the chapel were now dead. And yet the danger was far from over. Bolan watched as the detonator fell from the bomber's lifeless fingers to the tiled floor, skidding several feet before hitting the wall and bouncing back a few inches.

His Beretta in his right hand, he dove across the room, counting off the seconds as he flew through the air.

One thousand one...

Bolan hit the floor and snatched the detonator in one swift motion.

One thousand two...

He saw a series of buttons, but only one was illuminated. Did that mean it was the button that would halt the detonator or...? The Executioner had to make a lightning-fast decision. He had to take the chance.

MACK BOLAN ®
The Executioner

The Executioner®
Don Pendleton's

THROW DOWN

A GOLD EAGLE BOOK FROM

WORLDWIDE®

TORONTO • NEW YORK • LONDON
AMSTERDAM • PARIS • SYDNEY • HAMBURG
STOCKHOLM • ATHENS • TOKYO • MILAN
MADRID • WARSAW • BUDAPEST • AUCKLAND

Recycling programs
for this product may
not exist in your area.

First edition October 2012

ISBN-13: 978-0-373-64407-0

Special thanks and acknowledgment to
Jerry VanCook for his contribution to this work.

THROW DOWN

Printed in U.S.A.

Know thy self, know thy enemy. A thousand battles, a thousand victories.

—Sun Tzu

In every war, you must know your enemy, be cautious of your allies and never go against your gut—it is what will keep you alive.

—Mack Bolan

THE
MACK BOLAN
LEGEND

Nothing less than a war could have fashioned the destiny of the man called Mack Bolan. Bolan earned the Executioner title in the jungle hell of Vietnam.

But this soldier also wore another name—Sergeant Mercy. He was so tagged because of the compassion he showed to wounded comrades-in-arms and Vietnamese civilians.

Mack Bolan's second tour of duty ended prematurely when he was given emergency leave to return home and bury his family, victims of the Mob. Then he declared a one-man war against the Mafia.

He confronted the Families head-on from coast to coast, and soon a hope of victory began to appear. But Bolan had broken society's every rule. That same society started gunning for this elusive warrior—to no avail.

So Bolan was offered amnesty to work within the system against terrorism. This time, as an employee of Uncle Sam, Bolan became Colonel John Phoenix. With a command center at Stony Man Farm in Virginia, he and his new allies—Able Team and Phoenix Force—waged relentless war on a new adversary: the KGB.

But when his one true love, April Rose, died at the hands of the Soviet terror machine, Bolan severed all ties with Establishment authority.

Now, after a lengthy lone-wolf struggle and much soul-searching, the Executioner has agreed to enter an "arm's-length" alliance with his government once more, reserving the right to pursue personal missions in his Everlasting War.

Prologue

February 20, 2003

The Iraqi dictator stared at the screen of his computer as he waited for the security program to kick in. He knew he was about to experience the most important online conference he had ever had. In fact, it was probably the most important meeting of any sort he had ever taken part in.

A moment later, the screen divided into thirds. First to come into focus was the left-hand side, where the Iraqi saw the face of Mohammed Parnian sitting at his desk in Damascus. Parnian was the Syrian president and, like the Iraqi, a Sunni Muslim. But he was of the Alawi sect, who approached the Creator directly rather than through angels or Muslim saints.

The Iraqi president hated the man. But at least he was Sunni.

The middle screen became clear and a similar picture emerged from Iran. The swarthy little man behind the desk wore a light colored suit with an open collar. Hamid Bartovi was, of course, a Shiite, and the Iraqi remembered the long war he had fought against this man's country during the latter part of the twentieth century. Neither had won, and many lives had been lost on both sides. But even though he was Shiite, he, too, was Muslim.

Finally, the right side of the screen came into focus. The man sitting behind this desk had huge jowls hanging from the sides of his jaws and black hair slicked back by a comb. He looked angry. But, the dictator reminded himself, Pancho Martinez *always* looked angry. His face couldn't be used to judge his mood. Martinez, the president of Venezuela, was not a Muslim of any sort. He claimed to be Christian, but the Iraqi dictator knew that was primarily for political reasons.

If truth be known, none the leaders who had gathered for this secured video conference were particularly religious. They used religion when it was practical and discarded it when it was not. They did, however, have two things in common.

They all loved power.

And they all hated the United States of America.

"Good afternoon, gentlemen," the Iraqi said in English— the only language all four of them spoke. "I trust things are going well for you."

"As well as can be expected," Bartovi said. "Under the current circumstances."

"Things are quiet at the moment," Parnian said.

"All is well here," Martinez reported. "Particularly compared to you and your country."

The Iraqi sat back. "Yes," he said. "These are dark times for us. The U.S. invasion is inevitable, I believe."

"And you can *never* win such a war," Parnian said. "You must face that fact."

"That fact, as you put it," the Iraqi admitted, "is exactly why I have called this meeting." He paused to take in a long breath, scratching his clean-shaven chin as he did so. "I must go into hiding, I am afraid."

"A wise choice," Bartovi said. "But for how long?"

"I do not know," the Iraqi said. "But if the United States is true to form, they will take over my country, claim victory, set up some puppet regime and then go home when their citizens grow tired of losing American lives. It could be a matter of months. Then again, it might be years."

"Vietnam taught them nothing," Martinez said. "They are still quick to stick their nose into the business of other nations. But they lack the resolve to stay in place long enough to achieve their beloved *democracy*." The Venezuelan curled his lips in distaste.

"They believe democracy should be forced upon the entire world," Bartovi proclaimed. "Even nations that have no desire for it. In that sense, they are as bad as the Soviet Union used to be in spreading communism."

"We can spend all day discussing politics if you like," Parnian said. "But it will do nothing to help our friend in Iraq." This time, it was the word *friend* that caught the dictator's ear. It seemed forced from the Iranian's lips. The Iraqi knew they were friends only in their opposition to the Western superpower.

"So," Martinez said. "How can we be of service to you during your last few days in office?"

The dictator sat quietly for a moment, then said, "I would like to send each of you some presents."

"And they are…?" Bartovi asked.

The dictator glanced at the side of his computer, assuring himself that the red security light was on and the meeting was being scrambled beyond anything the Americans might be able to piece together into coherence. "I must move out my weapons," he said. "To Syria and Iran, I would like to send my biological and chemical supplies." He paused again, taking in another breath. "For Venezuela, I have a very special gift."

"Special gift?" Martinez repeated.

"I have one nuclear warhead," the dictator said. "But no missiles that will reach the United States from Baghdad." He paused yet again, this time for dramatic effect. "Launched from your country, however, Señor Martinez, it is another story."

"Let us make sure we are all on the same page, as the infidel Americans say," Parnian murmured. "You are expecting *us* to enter into a protracted war with the United States?"

"Of course not," the Iraqi said quickly. "You would have no better chance of winning than I do." A certain sense of satisfaction flowed through him as he spoke the words. His colleagues had reminded him that his forces could never defeat those of the U.S. It was gratifying to remind them in turn that they could be no more successful than he. "What I would like you to do," he said, "is simply hide these weapons until it appears to the world that they never existed in the first place. When they have searched my country high and low and found nothing, the weapons of mass destruction, or WMDs, as their cowboy president loves to call them, will appear to have been nothing but a political ploy. Americans will believe their leader used them simply as an excuse to take over Iraq."

"And they will turn against him," Bartovi said, nodding on the screen. "The Americans are quick to do that."

"Exactly," the Iraqi said, and he found himself nodding, too. "And in the next election, they will vote for someone as different from their current president as possible."

All four men chuckled softly. "They always do," Parnian said. "Republican, Democrat, liberal, conservative. They bounce from one extreme to another, never happy with anyone they have elected."

"Precisely," the Iraqi leader said. "And I will wait them out. When they go home, I will emerge stronger than ever."

"If they do not find you first," Martinez stated, staring out from the screen. "If they do, you will be tried in the World Court in Geneva. And with all due respect, my fellow president, you will be found guilty and probably hanged."

A surge of fear washed over the Iraqi, but he pushed it to

the side. No one—not even the mighty Americans—would be able to ferret him out of hiding. Not here, in his own country.

The fear left his soul. For a moment, the possibility that his ego had overtaken his common sense replaced it, but he pushed that thought aside, as well.

"That will not happen," he said, staring at Martinez. "But just in case the million-to-one shot comes through, I would like you all to pass my gifts on to some of our other friends. Friends who do not have obvious borders, or buildings and cities that could be bombed in retaliation."

"You are speaking of al Qaeda," Parnian said.

"And Hamas and Hezbollah," Bartovi added.

"Indeed I am," the Iraqi said. "Not to mention the Taliban. In the unlikely event that I do die or am captured, I want *millions* of American lives taken in revenge."

For a moment, all four leaders were quiet. Then Martinez said quietly, "Send me your gift."

"And to us, ours," Parnian stated.

"We will comply with your wishes," Bartovi said. "And even after you return to power, we can make good use of your gifts. Or rather, as you said, our freedom-fighting associates can."

"It is time that the Middle East rose again," the Iraqi said. And quickly added, "With, of course, our South American friends."

"Then it is settled," Bartovi said. "We are ready for delivery as soon as you are able."

The Iraqi dictator smiled into the split screen of his computer. "They are already on their way," he said. "Good evening, gentlemen."

"Good evening," the other three men replied.

The Iraqi dictator reached up and tapped the button that shut down his computer. Then he sat back in his chair and found himself chuckling again.

The people of the United States were the smuggest human beings in the world, in his opinion. They would find that they were not as prepared to take over Iraq as they thought. He would disappear for the duration of the war—which would not last long, due to the Americans' impatience. And when they had left again he would reemerge stronger than ever.

The hunted dictator's chuckling became full-blown laughter. His plan was perfect.

What could possibly go wrong?

1

Mack Bolan had known it would be only a matter of time.

After all, what softer target could Islamic terrorists find than small, unguarded Christian churches?

The flutter of the helicopter blades above his head did little to drown out the gunfire Bolan heard below as Jack Grimaldi, Stony Man Farm's top pilot, paused the chopper in midair above the tiny Catholic church standing out strangely in the middle-income residential area. Bolan recalled what he'd been told during the short helicopter "hop" from Chicago to Detroit.

The Catholic chapel had been built with money, and on a vacant lot, donated by an elderly retired schoolteacher who had never married. Having no heirs, she had passed on what little there was of her estate to the Church, with the request that the chapel be built in the medieval style reminiscent of many small Catholic churches in Europe. Her specifications had been followed to the letter, according to Stony Man Farm's source of information, and Bolan was slightly surprised that the city had been willing to rezone the lot for the unusual building.

Looking down through the windshield of the whirlybird, Bolan counted an even dozen armed men hiding behind statues of saints and firing AK-47s. Others had entered the chapel and were shooting through broken stained glass windows.

They all appeared to be on the ground floor of the three-story building.

Atop the church, however, one side of the cross mounted on the steeple had been shot away. The sight caused Bolan, also known as the Executioner, to frown. Detroit Police cars and a pair of SWAT vans encircled the building. While some of the officers spoke into handheld walkie-talkies and cell phones, most were too busy returning fire toward the church. But surely none of them were such poor marksman that they had missed their targets by two stories.

"Bring her down another twenty feet or so, Jack," Bolan told his pilot and longtime friend. "If I'm going into this gun-fight I'd just as soon not start it with a broken leg."

"You got it, big guy," Grimaldi said, and reached for the control panel in front of him. Seconds later the helicopter began to drop through the air like a well-controlled butter-fly. As they descended, Bolan saw the reason for the shot that had hit the cross on the steeple.

It had not been poor marksmanship. From this new van-tage point, he could see that two of the terrorists had climbed all the way to the roof. Rather than blasting away with as-sault weapons, they were taking their time with bolt-action sniper rifles.

Bolan considered landing the chopper on the flat area of the church's roof. So far, the enemies below hadn't taken much interest in the helicopter. The cops, of course, wouldn't shoot at him or Grimaldi. And the terrorists had probably surmised that the unmarked aircraft was from a news channel. They wouldn't shoot, at least not until Bolan tipped his hand as an enemy combatant. Like all terrorists, they wanted all the news coverage they could get.

"Hold it here," the Executioner said as he strapped the bungee cord harness around his shoulders, waist, and up be-tween his thighs. The sharp cracks of rifle fire were becoming even louder. As Grimaldi continued to hover over the church, Bolan reached into one of the pockets of his stretchy, skintight black battle suit—known simply as a blacksuit—and pulled out his satellite phone. A moment later, he had tapped in the number to Stony Man Farm, the top-secret counterterrorist organization with which he maintained an "arm's length" working relationship.

At one point in his career, he had been the Farm's top agent. But Bolan was by nature a loner. And he had returned to his one-man war against evil in all its forms, while remaining on professional and friendly terms with Stony Man Farm.

The telephone call bounced off several satellites, via phony phone numbers, before reaching its destination. The few seconds that took were well worth it when weighed against the possibility of a criminal or terrorist group intercepting the call. In addition, every word Bolan spoke into the phone, and every word spoken to him, would be scrambled beyond recognition to anyone who might have stumbled across the frequency.

Barbara Price, Stony Man Farm's chief mission controller, picked up the receiver. "Hello, Striker," she said, using the Executioner's mission code name. "Ten-twenty?"

"Hovering over the steeple right now," Bolan replied. "Getting ready to jump out to the end of this rubber band and engage in a little target practice." He paused, taking in a deep breath. "The only reason I called is to make sure word got to the cops that I'm on their side."

"That's been affirmed," Price said. "The local law enforcement forces are expecting a Fed to come falling from the sky."

"Good," Bolan said. "I just told Jack I didn't want to start this fight with a broken leg. I'm not too crazy about bouncing around on this bungee, either, while the cops below fill me with lead, like some monkey on a string."

"They won't," Price assured him. "If you get shot, it'll be by the bad guys."

Bolan chuckled softly. "That's a great consolation," he said with only a trace of sarcasm. "And we're sure the guys who've taken over the church are Hezbollah?" he added.

"Ninety-nine percent," Price replied. "That's what the informant was told, anyway."

For a brief moment, Bolan thought of the unusual set of circumstances that had brought him from the aftermath of an assault on the Chicago Mafia to Detroit. He had barely fired his final shot, ending the life and criminal career of the Windy City's godfather, when his satellite phone had vibrated, alerting him that there was trouble in Detroit and that Grimaldi would meet him at the airport in a helicopter. Hal Brognola, the director of sensitive operations at Stony Man Farm, had told him that a Catholic chapel in Detroit was under attack. The informant had said it was the work of Hezbollah—the terrorist group of which the man had once been a member.

The informant was a member no longer. He had been converted to Christianity by the Arabic-speaking priest of the chapel, and the terrorist group presently had a multimillion dollar contract out on his life. But he had not left Hezbollah before learning that they'd planned to place a bomb inside the chapel. And that they were going in heavy—with firepower—just in case they got caught during the act.

Which they had.

The new Arabic Christian had revealed this information during a confession to the priest, and since the crime had not yet taken place, and stood a chance of being prevented, Father Patrick O'Melton was not bound by the confidentiality code between clergyman and confessor. A former U.S. Army Ranger who had served his country during the First Gulf War, O'Melton had wasted no time contacting the authorities.

Bolan slid the single-point sling of his M-16 A-2 over his

shoulder. "See you later, Jack," he said as he opened the chopper door.

"I always *hope* so," Grimaldi replied.

The fall was short compared to a parachute jump, and before he knew it Bolan was reaching the end of the bungee cord and being jerked back up almost to the helicopter again.

The men on the ground floor were at no vantage point to fire at him as he sailed through the air once more, but the snipers atop the building had taken note of the chopper, and finally realized it was not from any news station. They turned their bolt action rifles his way, and a pair of "bees" buzzed past the Executioner as he continued to bounce. But the slow operation of the weapons kept the terrorists' fire to a minimum.

Twisting to face them on the end of the bungee, Bolan raised the M-16 A-2 in his right hand and cut loose with a 3-round burst of fire. The first round struck the bolt of a sniper rifle, sending up a flash of sparks from the weapon, and a scream from the mouth of the man holding it, as the .223 hollowpoint bullet split and struck his chest and abdomen. The second and third rounds took the sniper perfectly in the heart, and he fell forward onto his face with no further shrieks or cries of pain.

Bolan flipped the quick release snap on his bungee harness as the cord began to stabilize, and fell to the roof on his belly. With the M-16 in the prone position, he pressed the trigger again, and another trio of .223 rounds burst from the weapon, taking off the top half of the second sniper's head.

The Hezbollah man, wearing olive drab BDUs—battle dress uniform—like the rest of the terrorists Bolan had seen, didn't make a sound. He just stumbled a few feet backward, then toppled over the short retaining wall that surrounded the roof of the church. The last things Bolan saw of him were his boots as he fell "half-headed" over the side.

As the gunfire below him continued, the Executioner moved swiftly toward an open trapdoor near the center of the roof. Flipping the selector switch in his weapon to semi-auto, he stared down into the darkened hole.

Were the two men he'd just killed the only ones who had ascended from the bottom floor? There was no way of knowing. Other terrorists could be hidden within, waiting quietly for an assault from the roof.

There was only one way to find out.

Pulling a small ASP flashlight from another pocket of his blacksuit, the Executioner risked training a two-second beam of light down the steps. He saw and heard nothing. So, with the M-16 at the ready, he began to make his way down the stairs.

It took time for Bolan's eyes to readjust to the near darkness of the third floor of the chapel. But he waited, not wanting to risk giving away his position with another flash from the ASP. A small amount of light came down from the open trapdoor, so he moved to a corner of what appeared to be a Sunday school classroom. He was ninety-nine percent certain that no one was with him on the top floor of the chapel. But in case that one percent came through, he wanted the darkness to work *for* him rather than against him.

As soon as he could make out the blurry shapes of tables and chairs in the room, the Executioner glanced around. He saw no light switches or signs of electricity in any form. But on the tables, and built into the walls, were large candles and oil lamps. Moving toward the staircase in the middle of the room, he passed a large crucifix, then a painting of Jesus Christ with his hands folded in prayer. Continuing on toward a hallway and another set of steps, Bolan kept listening to the rifle rounds exploding below him. They had become more muffled since he'd entered the building, but were just as regular.

And, he knew, just as deadly.

When he reached the staircase, Bolan aimed his assault rifle downward and stared at the steps. The second floor of the small building seemed as deserted as the third, and he nodded to himself. The clock was ticking. There was a bomb somewhere inside the chapel. What kind of device, and how it was rigged to go off, had not been included in Brognola's brief. Bolan had barely had time to find out how Stony Man Farm's director had come across the intel in the first place.

He needed to talk to the priest and the converted Hezbollah man. This was a golden opportunity—a one-in-a-million chance to learn the ins and outs of what else the terrorist group had planned for the near future. But that was not the primary goal at the moment. Before he interviewed the informant and the priest, he needed to keep Saint Michael's Chapel from blowing up. And to do that meant both ridding the world of the terrorists on the ground floor and deactivating the bomb without destroying the chapel and the neighborhood surrounding it.

The Executioner's brain continued to roll near the speed of light. He suspected this was a fairly low-tech operation on Hezbollah's part. That meant that as soon as the terrorists began to think they were losing the gun battle, they would detonate the bomb by hand.

Slowly and quietly, Bolan began to descend the steps to the second floor. With each creak his boots made he paused, listening, to see if the men below had noticed it. But the gunfire continued, drowning out his quiet sounds on the stairs. Bolan realized the men below weren't likely aware that he'd taken out their two snipers. That meant he still had surprise on his side.

And he'd need it. He was vastly outnumbered, and surprise was the only advantage he would have in this ongoing firefight.

Reaching the second floor, Bolan saw that it was as deserted as the third, and he realized that the terrorists' plan for rifle fire had been as elemental as their plan for the bomb. Except for the two snipers he'd taken out on the roof, all of them were on the first floor.

Bolan halted his progress again, rapidly analyzing the situation. He could probably take out the men below by suddenly bounding down the final set of steps and launching a furious barrage of fire from the rear. But if he didn't get the individual in charge of the bomb, or if the explosives were connected to a dead man's switch, which would go off as soon as whoever was holding it relaxed his grip, Bolan might as well blow up the chapel himself.

He paused another moment before starting down the steps to the first floor. He had to admit, Hezbollah's attack might be low-tech, but it included a well-thought-out battle plan. Men who didn't mind dying, and thought it bought them a first-class ticket to paradise, held an incredible edge over warriors who were trying to kill the enemy and stay alive at the same time.

Bottom line in this situation was that the sooner Bolan wiped out all the terrorists on the first floor, the sooner the bomb would go off and destroy the chapel and probably the police officers surrounding it. Not to mention him.

He was fighting himself on this one.

THE CHAPEL WAS SMALL in comparison to most churches, and built of irregular stones that formed both the inside and the outside walls. One main room per story, with the staircase near the middle of each.

That meant that from where he stood presently, at the top of the steps, Bolan had a clear view of about half the ground level. The up side to this situation was his superior position. The down side was that many men firing out through the shattered stained glass windows could see him if they turned around.

And there were bound to be more Hezbollah out of sight behind the open staircase.

Luckily, the three men he could see were too engaged in their battle with the police to pay attention to their flanks or rear. So Bolan crept farther down the steps, the M-16 A-2 aimed and ready. He squatted momentarily, resting the rifle across his knees as he again sized up the situation. Blasts from the firearms of more men—unseen but heard—confirmed his suspicion that there were other terrorists at the rear. Exactly how many murderers there were in all was anyone's guess.

Squinting slightly, Bolan searched the men he *could* see for any sign of a bomb or a remote detonator. Several wore rucksacks, and such packs could hold anything from the most simple dynamite or nitroglycerine explosives to a small tactical nuclear device. But the scanty intel he had received from Brognola told him there was no nuke involved. Not in this strike, at least.

The Executioner took in a deep breath. At least that was *something*. He nodded to himself as the gunfire below continued. What he was facing was most likely plastic explosives—probably Semtex left over from the old Soviet Union that had found its way into Hezbollah hands. If he fired quickly on semiauto, he suspected he could put a .223 caliber hollowpoint round into the back of all six brains before whoever had the explosives even knew what was happening.

But what of the men he couldn't see, in the rear of the chapel? What if the bomb was with one of them? They would have more than enough time to see what had happened to their brothers in terror and detonate the explosive no matter how fast the Executioner descended the steps to take them on.

The gunfire both out and into Saint Michael's Chapel continued relentlessly. Through shattered remnants of stained

glass still stuck in corners of the windows, Bolan could see
dust floating through the outside air—the product of police
rounds striking the stones of the walls around the apertures.
As he continued to watch, one of the terrorists took a round
in the head and fell backward, dead on the cold stone floor.

That was good. But it didn't change things much for the
Executioner. Shooting two men and then turning toward the
rear of the building was hardly different from killing three.
The bomb would still have plenty of time to go off.

The unusual history of the antiquated chapel, and how out
of place it looked in the neighborhood, ran through the Executioner's mind once more. He was surprised that the city inspectors would have passed the candle and oil lamp lighting.
Even more remarkable was that the Detroit Fire Department
would have allowed a three-story structure to be built with
only one way up and down. The chapel would be a death trap
if any of the lamps or candles was ever mishandled.

The realization struck Bolan suddenly: the building inspectors might have insisted on a second escape route. One
he couldn't see. And medieval architecture was famous for
hidden rooms, staircases and tunnels.

Quickly and quietly, he rose to his feet. There was a second
way down; he could *feel* it. A route the terrorists would undoubtedly be unaware of, so that he could emerge suddenly,
with surprise on his side.

He just had to find it.

But time had become a factor, too. Every second he took
searching for the hidden route down was a second during
which the Hezbollah might decide that the gunfight had gone
on long enough. And that they should detonate the bomb.

The Executioner retraced his steps to the second floor and
moved away from the staircase. Crouching near a stone wall,
where he felt confident his whispers would not be heard by

the men below, he pulled out his satellite phone once more.
A few seconds later, he had Stony Man Farm on the line.

"Hal," Bolan said to Brognola. "I'm in a fix here. I can take
out the men in front of me. But if one of them isn't in control
of the bomb, then whoever is—that person being out of my
field of vision—is going to detonate it and bring this place
down as if it was built of straw instead of rock." He paused
a moment, taking a deep breath. "Do you have contact with
the priest and Hezbollah informant?"

"That's affirmative," Brognola said.

"This place is built to look like it came straight out of King
Arthur's court," Bolan said. "The only obvious way up and
down is the main staircase. But there's got to be another way
out. The fire inspectors would have never passed it if there
wasn't. What's more, I can *feel* it."

It was Brognola's turn to pause. Bolan knew the man was
thinking. And that what he had told him last meant the most
of all.

The director of sensitive ops never questioned the Executioner's battle instincts. He knew that if Bolan *sensed* there
had to be another set of stairs, there quite simply had to be
one.

"Hang on," Brognola said. "I've got the priest and his new
convert on the other line."

Bolan heard a click and found himself on hold. The gunfire below continued, and the seconds ticked away, feeling
like hours. He knew it was a strange and precarious predica-
ment they were in. The better the Detroit police did in this
gun battle, the closer they'd be to destroying the chapel and
themselves.

Finally, Brognola came back on the phone. "I just talked
to the priest," he said matter-of-factly.

"And?" Bolan answered.

"You're on the second floor now, right?"

"Right."

"Did you see a painting of Jesus and a crucifix on the wall?"

"I passed them on the way to the stairs," Bolan said. "There's an identical setup on the floor above me."

"Okay," Brognola said, and Bolan could practically see the chewed stub of the ever-present unlit cigar in the director's mouth. "The picture and the crucifix work in conjunction. Take the painting off the wall and set it on the floor."

Bolan slung the M-16 over his shoulder and turned to the wall. He lifted the painting of Christ off a nail and set it on the floor. "Done," he whispered into the phone.

"Good," Brognola said. "Now, go to the crucifix."

It took Bolan only two steps to reach the metal cross. "I'm there," he said quietly.

"The painting and the crucifix work together," the Stony Man Farm director said. "The painting acts as sort of a safety. Now that it's off the wall, twist the crucifix to the right."

Bolan reached out and grasped the bottom on the cross. "How far?"

"You'll know when you've gone far enough," Brognola answered.

Bolan twisted the crucifix. When it reached a 45-degree angle, a section of wall began to slowly swing backward, revealing an opening.

"You got it yet?" Brognola asked in Bolan's ear.

"Got it," he confirmed. He squinted into the dark opening. "I can just make out steps. Can you tell me where they come out on the ground floor?" As he waited for an answer, he slipped the sling off his shoulder and readied the M-16 in front of him.

"You'll exit in the middle of the bottom room," the Stony Man director said. "Facing the rear."

The exploding gunfire below had not let up as Bolan

stepped into the secret staircase and slowly descended. Brognola was still on the line as he did so. "Is there a peep-hole or anything like that, Hal?" he whispered into the satellite phone. "It'd be nice to get an idea what'll be in front of me when I come out of this thing."

"Sorry," Brognola said. "No 'coming attractions' on this one."

"Then tell me how to get out," Bolan said.

"A more simple setup, since it's hidden," Brognola said. "Just to the right of the exit you'll see a very modern-looking red button. Push it and the panel will open."

"I hope this one moves faster," he said, remembering how slowly the panel above had opened.

"I'm afraid not," Brognola grunted. "They were set up to satisfy the building code and for use in case of fire. No one had armed men and bombs on their minds when the place was built. I'm afraid it'll be just as slow."

"Okay," Bolan said simply. "Sometimes you have to go with what you've got. One more thing, though. You still have your informants on the other line? The priest and former Hez-bollah man?"

"I do."

"Ask them about the bomb itself," Bolan said. He stepped down onto a small landing, then turned to take the last set of steps. "I need to know for sure if there's a remote detonator, and especially if it has a dead man's switch. And ask our informant if there are any identifying features about the guy in charge of the bomb."

Bolan heard another click in his ear as Brognola put him on hold once more. He wondered briefly how long it would take for the men on the ground floor to realize what was going on once the panel began to swing open.

A few seconds later, the Stony Man director was back. "I'm afraid that's affirmative on both counts, big guy," he said. "Remote detonator and dead man's switch. The only *good* thing I can tell you is that there's a three-second delay between the time the bomber lets up on the button and when the explosives—it *is* Semtex, by the way—detonates. If you can get to it within that time frame and press the button again you'll be okay."

"How about the description of the bomber?" Bolan asked.

"Our new man here says he always wears a red-and-white-checkered scarf tied around his neck."

"Well, that's *something* at least," Bolan said. He had reached the bottom of the stairs and saw the red button glowing in the semidarkness. If he was lucky, the men he was about to face would be so intent on firing their weapons out the back that they wouldn't notice him immediately. He'd have to scan them as quickly as he could, find the one in the red-and-white scarf and kill the others before taking out the one with the dead man's switch.

Not to mention getting to the remote within three seconds.

"Okay, Hal," the Executioner said. "I'm ending this call now."

"Good luck," Brognola said. "Not that you've ever depended on luck."

Bolan didn't bother answering. He switched off the sat phone, stuck it back in his blacksuit, then reached up and pressed the red, glowing button with his index and middle fingers.

SURVIVAL OFTEN HINGED on decisions made at lightning speed and at the last possible second. Some men credited training for honing such decision-making. Others argued that nothing but *real live experience*—and luck in staying alive until that experience was obtained—was the key to success in life-and-death situations.

But a warrior such as the Executioner knew that neither

school of thought was completely right or completely wrong. And while it would be unlike Bolan to ever put such an idea into words, in his mind he knew that he fought out of instinct.

Vincent Van Gogh had been born a painter. Charles Dickens had been born a writer.

And in his very soul, Samuel Mack Bolan knew God had put him on this earth to be a fighter. His inborn talent was in taking up the slack when strong but vicious men of the world attempted to take advantage of their good but weaker brethren.

The wall creaked slightly, then began to move as Bolan made one of those last-minute decisions. This next step in saving Saint Michael's Chapel and the police officers surrounding it called for stealth. So before the panel had opened even an inch, he had set the M-16 down and drawn the sound-suppressed Beretta 93-R. Forgoing the use of the folding front grip on the machine pistol—Bolan knew his other hand had a far more important task to fulfill—he thumbed the selector switch from safety to semiautomatic.

The escape door had swung out another two inches when Bolan saw the first of the Hezbollah at the rear of the chapel, and snaked the Beretta through the opening to aim it at him. The man was wearing the same OD green BDUs as the terrorists he'd seen on the roof and at the front of the chapel. On his head was a dirty white turban that jerked slightly with each shot the man fired from his AK-47. There was no red-and-white scarf around his neck.

The panel had opened roughly four inches when Bolan depressed the Beretta's trigger and sent a subsonic 9 mm hollowpoint bullet from the barrel. The ignition made a soft, hissing sound, with the clank of the slide moving back and forth across the frame actually louder than the explosion itself. A thousandth of a second later, in addition to the BDUs and turban, the Hezbollah man wore something new.

A 9 mm hole in the back of his head.

The hidden staircase's panel continued to swing wider and Bolan thrust his arm through the opening. The man next to the one he had just killed wore a scarf around his neck, but instead of red-and-white it was solid black.

Had there been a mix-up in communication? Had the alleged Hezbollah-terrorist-turned-Christian gotten the color wrong? Bolan knew it was often little mistakes like this that determined the success or failure of a mission. But when he turned his focus to the man's hands, he saw they were wrapped around the pistol grip and fore end of another AK-47. And that sight caused him to pull the trigger once again, downing the man in the same fashion he had the first.

By this point, the door to the chapel was half open, and Bolan thrust his head around the still-moving panel. With a 180-degree view of the rear of the chapel, he spotted another terrorist to his far right—who *did* have on a red-and-white scarf. The man had noticed when his two comrades fell.

Bolan noted that in one hand, the terrorist held an old Soviet Makarov 9 mm pistol. But in the other was a device that looked little different than the remote control box for a television or a DVD player.

The Executioner had identified the bomber.

But there was a problem. There were still two Hezbollah firing out the broken windows at the other end of the room. And as quiet as the Beretta 93-R might be, they, too, had seen their brothers fall. The one nearest Bolan had begun to turn his way.

Bolan knew that as soon as he shot the man in the red-and-white scarf, he would have to dive forward to get to the dead man's switch. Such a task would leave him in no position to return fire. But if he shot the others first, the man with the Makarov would have more than enough time to sight him in and kill him with the Soviet pistol.

Either way, Bolan would be unable to get to the detonator. He'd likely be dead even before the bomb went off, killing everyone else inside the chapel, as well as many of the cops surrounding the structure.

His decision was made faster than he could measure. Bolan had two gunners about to shoot at him from the far windows, and only one—the man with the Makarov and detonator—at the other. Two men with assault rifles had a better chance of killing him than one with a pistol, so he turned the Beretta to his left. As he fired another quiet round from the 93-R, Bolan heard the Makarov explode, and felt a 9 mm round sear past his ear. With the nerves of steel for which he was famous, he stuck with his plan as that first round from the Beretta sent a hollowpoint slug through the temple of the man he'd aimed at.

The Makarov exploded again, and this time Bolan felt heat on his forehead as the bullet passed within millimeters of his face. Every survival instinct he had screamed for him to alter his plan of attack and spin toward the man with the detonator. But years of hard-core battle experience trumped those instincts, and the old adage *Never change horses in midstream* crossed his mind.

Bolan took careful aim and sent a 9 mm twisting through the brain stem of the man next to the one who had just fallen. Behind the terrorist, splatters of blood and gray brain matter flew out of the fist-size exit wound to splatter against the wall and out through the chapel's broken windows.

Another Makarov round caught the shoulder of Bolan's blacksuit, ripping it open. The skin beneath felt as if someone had held a lit kitchen match to it, but Bolan could tell no real damage had been done.

Finally swinging toward the terrorist in the red-and-white-checkered scarf, he found that the man had turned to face him. The Executioner could see his frustration. He had missed three shots at reasonably close range, and was trying to line up his sights to keep from missing again.

The Hezbollah's arm stopped in place just as Bolan swung the Beretta toward the red-and-white scarf. But the Executioner's finely focused brain told him it was of no use. He was a microsecond behind the terrorist, who was carefully using the sights and this time would not miss.

A split second later, the man squeezed the trigger.

And Bolan heard a metallic clink as the hammer fell on an empty pistol.

The Executioner wasted no time. The Hezbollah bomber had run his weapon dry shooting from the windows, and had used his final three 9 mms trying to get Bolan. That was his bad luck. And Bolan was determined to make sure that bad luck stayed on the terrorist's side.

Flipping the selector switch to 3-round burst, he sent a trio of rounds at the man's chin and eyes. The Hezbollah terrorist flopped back against a shattered church window like a spineless rag doll as blood, gray matter and bits and pieces of skull flew out the back of his head.

All the terrorists at the rear of the chapel were dead.

But the danger was far from over.

Bolan watched as the detonator was jarred from the bomber's lifeless fingers. It hit the floor, skidding several feet across the slick tile before hitting the wall and bouncing back a few inches.

Bolan kept the Beretta in his right hand as he dived across the room like a wide receiver going after a pass with too much lead from the quarterback. As he flew through the air, he counted off the seconds in his mind.

One thousand one...

The Executioner hit the floor and snatched the detonator off the tile in one swift motion, turning it face-up in order to read it.

One thousand two...

As he lifted the instrument to his eyes, he saw a series of numbers, with only one illuminated. Bolan had no idea if the light meant that button would halt the detonator or not. But he had to make another lightning-fast decision, and take a chance.

He pressed the button with his thumb and continued to count.

One thousand three...one thousand four...

He counted all the way to ten before allowing himself to feel certain the bomb would not go off. For most men, it would have been the longest ten seconds of their lives. Bolan had faced similar danger more times than he could recall, so it wasn't the longest ten seconds, but it had to be close.

Finally looking up from the detonator, he saw the bomb itself for the first time. The Hezbollah had made no attempt to hide it; it had been placed against the back of the staircase, where Bolan had been unable to see it, coming out of the secret passageway. From where he presently sat, with his back against the wall, he could tell it was a relatively simple device constructed of Semtex, as he'd guessed it would be. He shook his head slightly, realizing he had passed within inches of it when he'd emerged from the hidden door.

Bolan stared at the bomb. He suspected he could disarm it himself if he had time. But he *didn't* have time. He could still hear rifle fire from the front of the chapel, which reminded him that the battle was not yet over. There were still five men out there, doing their best to kill the SWAT officers and other cops on the street. Since he had control of the detonator, it made more sense to eliminate all the Hezbollah terrorists and leave the bomb neutralization to the Detroit PD bomb squad.

He paused a moment, listening and thinking. Luckily, there was no indication that the terrorists out front had taken notice of what happened behind them.

Bolan's eyes rose slightly and he saw yet another crucifix on the wall, just above the body of the last man he had shot before going after the terrorist with the red-and-white scarf and the detonator. Was it truly *luck* that had kept the other men from noticing as he took out the bomber and the rest of the gunners at the back? Or was there indeed something more powerful working for him, here in Saint Michael's Chapel?

Bolan didn't know the answer to that. But he *did* know—deep in his soul—that if a force greater than he was guiding him, that force expected him to utilize the talents he'd been given to neutralize this situation.

The Executioner picked the Beretta up off the floor, dropped the partially spent magazine and replaced it with a full box mag from one of the carriers on the shoulder holster beneath his right arm. He had more work cut out for him. And it would have to be done one-handed if he wanted to keep the detonator depressed. He reached up and felt the torn cloth of the blacksuit on his shoulder. The skin beneath it still burned, but no real damage had been done. He thought of the three rounds the man in the red-and-white scarf had fired at him. He had missed all three times—at relatively close range. Most rookie cops could have put those rounds into the X ring of a silhouette target their first time at the shooting range.

And then, when the man finally did take his time and line up the sights, he had run the Makarov dry.

Again, Bolan had to wonder if there wasn't something more than so-called luck at work here within the chapel.

Bolan cleared his mind. The time for action was at hand; there would be opportunity for philosophical reflection later. No more stealth now; a hundred percent full-court press was needed to eliminate the Hezbollah terrorists at the front of the chapel. And Bolan could not allow himself to be killed or disabled while doing so. The bomb would go off just as surely as if he had dropped the detonator after taking out the man in the red-and-white scarf.

Drawing the mammoth .44 Magnum Desert Eagle from his hip holster, Bolan kept the remote button depressed with his middle finger, and used his index finger and thumb to pull the slide back just far enough to make sure a copper jacket was chambered in the barrel. Then he flipped the safety off with his thumb.

And with the Desert Eagle in his right hand, the remote "dead man" detonator in his left, he started toward the front of the chapel.

COMPARED TO WHAT HE'D already been through, the rest of the battle seemed like a cakewalk.

When Bolan emerged from the side of the staircase, he saw that the police out front had found their mark on yet another of the Hezbollah men shooting back at them. A terrorist with long black hair, partially covered by a green baseball cap, lay facing away from the windows. The corpse's hands were still wrapped around his throat in what had proved to be a vain attempt to curb the blood flow brought on by the round that had sliced through his carotid artery. His BDU blouse was soaked with blood, and what had undoubtedly been a gusher not unlike a freshly tapped oil well had subsided into a mere trickle of red running down his neck.

The man's caramel-colored skin had turned white in death.

Bolan dragged his eyes away from the body. Two of the six terrorists were down. That meant four more needed killing.

Taking his time, Bolan raised the Desert Eagle and aimed it at the back of the head of the man on the far left of the row of windows, then tapped the trigger. The Desert Eagle exploded, far louder than the 7.62 mm rifle rounds going the other way. And as it hit its mark, it drew the attention of the Hezbollah men still engaged in the gun battle.

All three turned as one.

Bolan swung the Magnum right, firing a round into the face of a man wearing a checkered kaffiyeh. The blast made the tail of the headdress blow back as if caught in the wind, and the features of his face disintegrated into a mass of blood, muscle and bone.

Bolan's attack was little different from a bowling pin pistol match, in which competitors kept swinging to the right in order to knock over the wooden pins. Bolan did so again, and the shot he aimed at the next terrorist caught the man in the throat as he attempted to rise from where he'd been firing out of the window.

The round went between the carotid artery and the jugular vein and took out his larynx. He coughed and sputtered spasmodically as his chest jerked in and out. He would die from the wound, Bolan knew. But he might not die fast enough to keep him from returning fire if Bolan moved on. So, as AK-47 fire from the last terrorist began to whiz past him, Bolan put another round between the choking man's eyes.

That .44 Magnum ended the choking and coughing. For eternity.

Bolan swung the Desert Eagle toward the last man, who had, like the bomber with the Makarov, suddenly run his weapon dry. But you could tell the terrorist was a practiced warrior in the smooth way he dropped the empty mag and reached for a full one in the sash tied around his waist. He was fast.

But the Executioner was faster.

Bolan sent a double-tap of .44 Magnum rounds into the man's chest, and the magazine fell from his left hand, the rifle from his right. He collapsed onto the floor, which had become a mass of OD green BDU uniforms soaked black, and several ever-growing pools of bright red blood.

Rounds were still exploding from the police outside the

chapel. But they began to slow as no more return fire flew back at them from within Saint Michael's.

Bolan pulled out his satellite phone and tapped in the number to Stony Man Farm. "Let them know it's all over in here, Hal," he said into the instrument. "Tell them I've got the detonator and it needs to be turned over to the bomb squad."

"Great work as always," Brognola said. "Anything else I should tell them?"

"Yeah," Bolan said drily. "Tell them not to shoot the big guy in the stretchy blacksuit."

The Executioner ended the call. Two minutes later, SWAT teams and explosive experts had entered the chapel. Bolan carefully turned the detonator over to the captain in charge of the bomb squad as other members of his team removed the bomb itself and gingerly carried it out to their van.

2

The hotel room on the third floor of Detroit's downtown Hilton looked no different from thousands of others across the globe. It contained two double beds separated by a nightstand and lamp, with a Gideon Bible tucked in a drawer. At the foot of the beds, centered along the wall, was a wooden desk and chair. The bedspreads were generic, as were the pictures hanging on the cream-colored walls.

The room looked much like all the others weary travelers occupied the world over.

What *was* different were the occupants.

Bolan had changed out of his combat blacksuit while still at Saint Michael's, using a downstairs closet for privacy. He now wore khaki slacks, a navy blue blazer, a white shirt open at the collar, and black-and-oxblood saddle shoes. For all the world to see, he appeared to be just another businessman who had taken the liberty of removing his necktie and folding it into a pocket of the blazer.

What could not be seen, however, were the weapons beneath that sport coat. The sound-suppressed Beretta 93-R was once again fully loaded, with the first round already chambered and the selector switch thumbed to safe. Opposite it in the leather-and-nylon shoulder rig hung an extra pair of 15-round 9 mm magazines, with subsonic loads that also helped keep the weapon down to a whisper when he pulled the trigger.

Almost in direct contrast to the Beretta was the bigger pistol he wore on his right hip. The Desert Eagle sounded like a nuclear bomb when it went off inside a building, and not much quieter outside. The .44 Magnum was loaded with 240-grain semijacketed hollowpoint rounds, and extra box mags for it were secured behind Bolan's left hip.

In addition to the big firearms, he carried a North American Arms .22 Magnum, rimfire, single-action mini-revolver in the right pocket of his blazer. The tiny firearm could be hidden in the palm of Bolan's big fist or secreted in any number of other places around his body, as the situation called for. At the moment, it was doing double duty as a "last ditch" backup, and also as a weight that allowed the tail of his jacket to be swept back from his side, for a lightning-fast draw of the Desert Eagle.

Bolan's final weapon was the newly manufactured Spyderco Navaja. With the ancient Spanish navajas—sometimes known as "caracas" due to their ratcheting sound when opened—as its prototype, the Spyderco was an updated, four-inch-blade version built with the latest innovations in steel and technology.

Bolan had found the Spyderco folder with its one-handed opening hole to be an indispensable tool, and sometimes weapon.

He sat on the edge of the bed closest to the door, facing a man who was just as unique, in his own way, in the cookie-cutter motel room. Father Patrick O'Melton wore a black suit and cap-toed black dress shoes. But above the equally dark tunic, his white Catholic priest's collar stood out in bold relief. His sandy-red, wavy hair had been combed straight back, barely covering the tips of his ears at the sides. The priest's nose appeared to have been broken more than once, and a long scar, almost as white as his collar, extended from his left ear down the side of his face to his chin, parting the short, stubby beard that covered the rest of his jaw.

The two men had just entered the room and sat silently for the few seconds it took to check each other out. Bolan, never known to beat around the bush, broke the silence. "My people tell me you were a U.S. Army Ranger."

O'Melton nodded slowly and his lips curled into a small smile. "That's right," he said pleasantly. "First Gulf war. I got to sneak around Baghdad dressed like an Iraqi, and help guide our missiles and bombers onto target."

Bolan tapped his throat, then gestured to the priest's collar. "This was a pretty dramatic career change, wouldn't you say?"

"Oh, it was dramatic," O'Melton agreed, his head still bobbing. "But not as strange as it might seem at first."

When Bolan didn't respond, the priest went on. "It was toward the end of the war," he said. "When Saddam Hussein was pulling his troops back to Iraq and setting fire to all the oil wells he could on the way. The deciding moment wasn't all that colorful, I'm afraid. I just pretty much thought okay, you've killed a lot of bad guys, and that was what you were supposed to do. But now it's time to do your best to save some."

Bolan finally nodded in understanding. He leaned forward slightly, clasped his hands together and said, "Tell me about this snitch of yours."

"He's a diamond in the rough," O'Melton said. "Former Hezbollah terrorist. He knows a lot of the ins and outs of the organization—but not everything, of course. Each cell in each terrorist organization—Hezbollah, al Qaeda, or any of the others—operate on a need-to-know basis, just like a lot of our own intelligence agencies. But my man says he's willing to help."

"How'd he come to tell you about the attack on Saint Michael's?" Bolan asked.

"He told me in confession," the priest said. "And since it was a crime that hadn't yet occurred, I wasn't bound to the confidentiality pact. In fact, I was bound by law to report it." Father O'Melton held a fist to his mouth and coughed slightly.

"He was in confession," Bolan said. "Are you telling me that he's given up Islam for Christianity?"

"That's what he told me."

"Well, his intel was great," the soldier said. "The attack on the chapel came off just as he told you it was going to. If the Detroit PD hadn't gotten advance notice, instead of a few dozen bullet holes in the walls, your chapel wouldn't even be standing now."

"He was on the money right down to the tiniest detail," O'Melton agreed.

"And he's willing to help us go after Hezbollah and other terrorists, as well?"

"That's what he said."

For a moment, the two men fell silent, staring into each other's eyes. But Bolan hadn't missed the slight tone of voice change, or the ambiguity, in two of Father O'Melton's answers. When he asked if this snitch had converted to Christianity, instead of a simple yes, the priest had said, "That's what he told me." And when questioned about the informant's willingness to help, O'Melton had answered, "That's what he said."

Father O'Melton might be a man of God, but he wasn't naive by any means. He knew what double and even triple agents were made of, and that there was always the possibility his informant was trying to play him and the feds rather than help them.

Bolan finally broke the silence again. "There's something in how you're answering my questions, Father. The tone of your voice. And the fact that your answers come in sort of a neutral way, such as 'that's what he told me' instead of just a simple 'yes.'"

"I'm just reporting to you as best I can," O'Melton said.

"That's good," Bolan stated. "But there's one thing that bothers me."

"It bothers me, too," the priest said. "Christianity and Islam are similar in some ways, but quite different in others. For a Christian to deny Christ is a mortal sin. But Muslims are allowed to masquerade as Christians or Jews or anything else they find advantageous in order to further their Islamic jihad." He paused to cough again, then said, "The typical American—and I might also include the typical American Christian—either doesn't know that or chooses to ignore it. But it's right there in black-and-white in the Koran."

Bolan nodded. "I've read it."

O'Melton smiled again, but this time looked more sad and weary. "What that means for us," he said, "is that if we use this guy, we can never be sure we can trust him until the op is completed."

Bolan leaned back on the bed. "You say 'us,'" he said. "What exactly do you mean by that?"

"I want to go with you," O'Melton said. "I feel a calling to help. I speak reasonably good Arabic and Farsi. And I'm well-trained to assist you, both in combat and in helping interpret any theological leads that might come up."

"The heavens didn't open this time, either, I'm guessing," Bolan said.

O'Melton threw back his head and laughed. "No, again it wasn't that dramatic. Just a feeling God's given me. Like maybe this was my calling all along—to be trained as an Army Ranger, then go to seminary for training as a priest, then combine the two in order to help save the world from… well, who knows what?"

The Executioner sat quietly for a moment. If Father O'Melton could remember what it was like to use a gun, he might indeed be valuable during this mission. And what, exactly, was that mission? Bolan wondered. At this point, it was to meet the priest's informant and run him for all he was worth, taking out every Hezbollah terrorist or other threat to the world until they'd exhausted the man's use.

But Bolan was getting his own "feelings" at the moment. And one of them told him that this could turn into a much larger operation than they were able to see at the moment.

He sat up straight again. "Well," he said, "let's take your man and go with him. Where is he?"

The priest didn't answer verbally. He just stood up and walked to the side of the room. Bolan had noticed that they were in a connecting room when he'd first entered. He watched O'Melton unlock their side of the twin doors and rap his knuckles on the other.

A moment later, that door opened, too.

And standing in the doorway, Bolan saw one of the scruffiest looking men he'd ever seen.

ZAID AHMAD WAS PERHAPS five feet five inches tall if he stood on his toes and stretched his neck as high as it would go. Bolan estimated he'd tip the scales at a hundred forty pounds—if the dirty BDUs he wore were soaking wet. Ahmad sported long hair like some young prophet from another century, and his beard looked to be at least a foot long. Both hair and beard were just beginning to sparkle with tiny patches of white.

Father O'Melton stepped back and let the man shuffle across the carpet.

Ahmad's dark brown eyes darted nervously from the priest to Bolan and then around the room. The Executioner didn't blame him. Brognola had already told him that Hezbollah knew Ahmad had turned on them and even tipped the authorities off about Saint Michael's. So the swarthy little man had a price on his head. In fact, he was probably number one on the Islamic hit list.

O'Melton took the frightened man's arm and guided him toward the desk, pulling out the chair and turning it around so he could sit down. Ahmad did so, then leaned forward with his hands folded and his arms between his legs, looking as if he was trying to further shrink his already diminutive size.

Bolan had seen such behavior thousands of times in the past. Even when the subject wasn't obsessing on it, his subconscious mind always held the knowledge that he might already be marked for death. In this case, Ahmad's body language suggested that he was trying to make himself the smallest target he possibly could.

Of course, there was another viable answer to the man's nervous demeanor. He might just be one heck of a good *actor*.

"Let's start at the beginning," Bolan said. "What do you want me to call you?"

"Zaid is my first name. Ahmad my second. Please choose whichever one you like."

"Okay, Zaid," Bolan said. "Father O'Melton tells me you've turned to Christianity."

For a second, the informant's eyes lit up. "Yes," he said. "I have accepted Jesus Christ as my personal savior."

Bolan continued to stare into the man's face. "What caused this drastic change?" he asked.

"In addition to the Koran," Ahmad said. "I began to read the Bible. Especially the New Testament. I cannot explain it to you any more than I was able to explain it to Father O'Melton, but a change came over me. And I recognized the writings of Paul the Apostle and the other writers as the word of God."

Bolan waited while the man in the desk chair caught his breath. Then he said, "Who all knows about your conversion? Your Hezbollah buddies?"

"I have heard that they do," Ahmad said. "At least the Hezbollah men here in the U.S., on assignment with me. I have even heard that there is a bounty out on my head. I fear I would be killed immediately if they find me."

"So how is it you were allowed to stay away from Saint Michael's during the attack?" Bolan asked.

"I *wasn't*," Ahmad replied. "I was dressed and ready. I even entered the chapel with the other men. But in the confusion that followed, I was able to sneak back out and get away."

Bolan's eyebrows lowered. The story had holes in it big enough to ride a camel through. "So explain to me how it was that, if they knew you'd changed sides, they allowed you to come along on this strike. And tell me how you got away." He stared deeply into the man's dark eyes, looking for any sign of deception. "I'm assuming you had on the BDUs you're still wearing, and were armed."

"I had a pistol belt, extra ammo and an AK-47," Ahmad said.

"And you're telling me that with all the hoopla going down at the chapel, nobody—not just your own Hezbollah team—"

"My *former* Hezbollah team," Ahmad interrupted.

"Okay, *former* team. How is it that none of them, or any of the cops who'd already arrived at the scene, saw you sneak back out of the chapel in full terrorist battle gear?"

Father O'Melton cleared his throat. "I can answer that," he said. "I was waiting for him a block away in my car."

That statement made Ahmad's story a lot more plausible. Not a lot. But some.

"So you think you can still help us with future Hezbollah strikes?" Bolan asked.

"I do," the man in the green BDUs said. "That is, if the suspicions the Hezbollah men had about me died here, with them. If they didn't pass them on before the gunfight."

"I'm assuming you mean other Hezbollah cells back in

Lebanon and Syria," Bolan said. "But even if word never left the men who died here today, how are you going to explain to your people back home that you survived the attack on the chapel when all the other men died?"

"By telling the *truth,*" Ahmad said. "Or at least part of it."

Bolan's eyebrows furrowed even deeper. "I think you'd better explain a little more, Zaid."

"I will contact another Hezbollah cell and tell them I pretended to convert to Christianity to further the jihad," he said. "And that a priest helped me escape." For the first time, a smile crossed the man's face. "They will think it's hilarious."

"That sounds like it might just work," Bolan said. "But I've got one more question for you."

"Please ask it," Ahmad prompted.

"How am I supposed to know which side you're really on?"

A long and uneasy silence filled the room. It was clear that Ahmad knew as well as Bolan did that it was impossible to be certain of where his true loyalties lay. Finally, the little man cleared his throat and said, "All I can do is tell you that I believe Jesus, born to a virgin, was God on earth," he said. "But he was also a man—a man who resisted all temptation from Satan and lived a sinless life. I believe he was crucified to pay for the sins of all who accept him, and that on the third day he arose from the dead."

Bolan continued to stare at the man. He knew no more than he had before Ahmad's last speech. The little Hezbollah man could have read the New Testament, just as Bolan and O'Melton had read the Koran, and learned exactly what he was supposed to say if he was pretending to be a Christian.

It could all be a ruse. And only time, and Ahmad's actions in the operation they were about to undertake, would prove he was telling the truth or lying.

"Okay," Bolan said. "Assuming you're on the level, what can you tell me about upcoming Hezbollah activities?"

Ahmad seemed to shrink even smaller in his chair and his eyes flittered around the room once more, as if he was afraid someone besides Bolan and the priest might hear. When he spoke, it was in a whisper. "Ever since the death of Osama bin Laden, all Islamic jihad organizations have been aching to hit the U.S. with a strike that exceeds the World Trade Center and Pentagon attacks."

"Has Hezbollah united with al Qaeda?" Bolan asked.

"No," Ahmad said. "There are too many philosophical differences between the two groups." He paused, then took in a deep breath. "The fact is, the two hate each other."

"They just hate America more," Father O'Melton interjected.

"'The enemy of my enemy is my friend,'" Bolan quoted.

"Precisely," Ahmad said. "But as far as I know, there are no joint operations currently being planned."

"So just tell us what you *do know*," Bolan said.

"I cannot tell you the details of any small future strikes such as the chapel," he said. "We were never given details until the last minute. But I do have information that I believe will help America, and Christians and Jews throughout the world." When he drew in a breath this time, the long shaggy tails of his mustache were sucked into his mouth along with the air. Carefully, he pulled them back out with a thumb and forefinger. "There are things being planned that are far bigger and more destructive than the attack on the chapel. Things that will make the World Trade Center and Pentagon attacks pale in comparison."

"Give them to me in a sentence or two," Bolan said. "Then I want you to go down to the barbershop in the lobby. I want your hair cropped short and your beard gone." He stood up and stretched his back. "If you're going to be running with us, you need to look like us. And while all the Hezbollah men in your cell are now dead, there's always a chance we'll run into some other terrorist who recognizes you."

Ahmad just nodded.

"So tell me what you know," Bolan said.

"I know that Saddam Hussein *did* have weapons of mass destruction," the little man on the desk chair said. "But he had time to ship them out of Iraq to sympathetic and allied countries before the United States invaded."

For a moment, the Executioner was struck silent. He had expected Intel, but nothing this big. "Do you know what they were and where they went?" he asked.

"There were large stores of chemical and biological weapons, and one medium-range rocket with a nuclear warhead."

"Tell me," Bolan said, with a trace of suspicion in his voice. "How does a Hezbollah soldier such as yourself come by such 'inside' information?"

Ahmad shrugged. "For many years now, Hezbollah has transported both weaponry—rifles, ammunition and the like—as well as documents from Iraq to Syria and back. We did not always know what we were delivering. It is one of the duties we perform in return for the protection both countries provide for us." He stopped speaking for a moment, then said. "Allow me to rephrase that last part. My English is not always so good, and I should have spoken in the past tense. These jobs are done in exchange for the protection both countries provide for my *former comrades* in Hezbollah. In any case, as you might guess with any peoples, rumors abound under such conditions. I cannot be certain, but I suspect Syria took possession of large quantities of biological or chemical agents. My reasoning for this is that only a few days before the U.S. invaded Iraq, we drove the largest and longest convoy of supply trucks we had ever taken from Iraq to Damascus."

"And you had no idea what you were carrying?" Bolan asked.

"Not officially," Ahmad said. "But it did not take an Albert Einstein to make an educated guess. There were many fifty-five gallon barrels in the trucks—all unmarked. They looked identical to the drums that contained the chemical weapons Saddam used on Iran during their war, then later on his own Kurdish people."

"Do you still have contacts in Iraq and Syria?" Bolan asked.

"Yes," Ahmad said. "At least I *think* I do. Once again, it depends on whether or not word of my conversion was sent back overseas."

Bolan motioned for Ahmad to stand up, and he complied. "We'll get into the details in a little while," he said. Bolan reached into his pocket and produced a roll of hundred-dollar bills. He dealt off several like a blackjack dealer in Las Vegas, then shoved them into the man's hand. "As for now, go downstairs to one of the shops in the lobby and buy some American-looking clothes. We can't have you running around here in dirty BDUs. But don't throw away your kaffiyeh or turban, or anything else you wear at home. We'll need that look on you when we get there."

"Where are we going?" he asked.

Bolan reminded himself that Ahmad had still not proved his trustworthiness. So far, he was all talk. "I'll let you know when the time comes," he said simply. Bolan returned the rest of the money to his pocket as the man left the room and entered the hall.

As soon as Ahmad was out of earshot, Bolan turned back to Father O'Melton. "I'd like to know a little more about you, Father," he said. "You're hardly the run-of-the-mill Irish-American Catholic priest. So could you explain why you're here in this room instead of comforting the parishioners whose chapel was just attacked?"

O'Melton smiled, and the gleam in his eyes told Bolan this

wasn't the first time he'd been asked such a question. "Like I told you," he said. "I was a U.S. Army Ranger before becoming a priest."

Bolan nodded, continuing to stare the man in the eye. But O'Melton's gaze was almost as firm. "And I've told you what I did during the first Gulf War," he said. "Undercover in Baghdad, and wrapped up in all the Moslem trappings I could find to hide my pale Irish skin. Even used that spray-on tan stuff some actors wear."

"You guys did a good job bringing in the smart bombs," Bolan said.

O'Melton grinned slightly. "Were you there?" he asked.

Bolan let a smile curl the corners of his mouth. "Not officially," he said. "But yeah, I was there."

"I thought you must have been," the priest said. "I was outside Saint Michael's with the SWAT teams and cops when you bounced down onto the roof on the end of that big rubber band. Then you systematically engineered the retaking of the chapel practically alone. I can't imagine our government not using a man with your abilities in *any* war or conflict which came up."

"Thanks for the compliment," Bolan said. "But we're here to talk about you, not me. So, how'd you go from Ranger fatigues to that white collar? The whole story."

O'Melton let out a loud laugh that had to have come from the pit of his stomach. "It's difficult to explain to most people," he said. "But, like I already said, I got a calling from God."

Bolan waited silently for him to continue.

O'Melton smiled genuinely. "Don't worry—I'm not crazy. The clouds didn't part and I didn't hear any voice or anything. Fact is, I was on the phone, guiding a USAF sortie to its target, when I suddenly got a feeling more weird than anything I'd ever experienced in my life."

The Executioner leaned forward. "That you shouldn't be helping kill your fellow man?"

"No," the priest said. "Not at all. It was a feeling that I was doing *exactly* what I was supposed to be doing with my life at that moment. That I was doing *exactly* what God had put me on this planet to do. But with that knowledge came another feeling—that it wasn't *all* God had planned for me. A feeling that there would be a major change in my life as soon as the war was over and I got back stateside."

"The knowledge that you should become a priest?" Bolan asked.

"No, not yet." Father O'Melton crossed his legs on the bed opposite Bolan before he continued. "You need to know a little back story on me first, before I go on. You see, before all of this happened, I'd planned on making the Army my career. I was hoping to go from the Rangers to Delta Force. To me, up until then, that seemed like the ultimate goal I could achieve."

"So what changed that goal so drastically?"

"Another feeling," O'Melton said. "And I'm sorry but it wasn't any more outwardly dramatic or theatrical than the one I'd had in Baghdad. What happened was that as I was coming down the steps of the transport plane when I got back home, I looked into the crowd that was there to greet us, and saw an elderly priest near the front of the pack. He didn't say anything to me. Our eyes didn't even meet. I just saw him and suddenly *knew* that my Army days were over, and as soon as my enlistment was up, I'd be heading for a seminary."

Slowly, Bolan nodded in understanding. He had experienced a similar "calling" years before, when he first realized it was his duty to fight evil in whatever form it attacked. "So you went from warrior to priest," he finally said.

O'Melton grinned again. "I suppose you could say that." Grabbing the lapel of his suit jacket with his left hand, he pulled it back to expose a Smith & Wesson, 5-shot, Chiefs

Special .357 Magnum revolver in a well-worn, brown leather shoulder holster. "I prefer to think of it more like I went from being a simple warrior to being a *Christian* warrior," he said, as his jacket fell back into place.

The priest held a fist to his mouth and coughed. Then he continued. "Now, the next thing people usually ask me about when I tell them all this is what Jesus said about 'turning the other cheek.' I agree with that, of course. But I interpret it to mean that you shouldn't retaliate to an insult, or a minor attack that would stop on its own. Like a slap." He paused a moment, then went on. "What people forget is that Jesus also said, 'Let him who has no sword sell his cloak and buy one.' You can look it up if you want to. Luke 22:36. Jesus, you see, knew the difference between an insult and a deadly attack, and he knew his disciples would be violently opposed when they set out to spread the word about him after he'd ascended to heaven."

Bolan had been listening, and now said, "Okay, then, Father. What—"

O'Melton interrupted him. "Just call me Pat, if you would. When the gunfire starts on this mission we're about to undertake, it'll be a lot faster and easier."

"That answers the question I was about to ask," Bolan said. "What role do you see yourself playing from here on in?"

"I'm supposed to go with you and help you," the priest said simply.

"Another one of those 'feelings'?" Bolan asked.

O'Melton nodded. "Just as strong as the others I mentioned. That's what God has me here for. He saw to it that I was trained as a Ranger *and* in the seminary. And now these two diverse forms of education are coming together to complete the Lord's plan."

Bolan hesitated a moment. "Okay then…Pat. It won't hurt to have somebody watching my back. And I could do a lot worse than a former Army Ranger." His eyes strayed from the priest's face to the shoulder where the small revolver was hidden. "We might want to upgrade your armament a little, though."

"Suits me fine," O'Melton said. "Small arms were one of my specialties."

Bolan pointed past the desk, toward the corner of the room where he had dropped his suitcases and equipment bags. "Look through the stuff in there, Pat," he said. "Take what you think you'll need, and don't be timid. If there's anything you want that I don't have, I can get it for you. While you're doing that, I've got a call to make."

As Father O'Melton began sorting through the guns, knives and other items in the black nylon ballistic bags, Bolan sat back down on the bed and pressed the satellite phone to his ear. A moment later, he had Barbara Price on the line. "I'm going to have Jack fly us back to Stony Man Farm in his chopper," he said. "In the meantime, get a plane ready to take us overseas."

"That's affirmative, Striker," Price said. "Anything else you'll need?"

"Yeah," Bolan said. "I've got all of my alternate ID with me. But we're going to need two extra sets. Passports, driver's licenses and some phony family photographs and other simple things that tend to confirm an identity." He described Father O'Melton and Zaid Ahmad in detail. "We'll get their photos just as soon as we land, before we transfer to the plane."

"I'll have the aircraft fueled, checked and ready," Price said. "What's your destination?"

Bolan hesitated for a second. Then he said simply "Damascus," and pressed the button ending the call.

3

Damascus, Syria, was known as the oldest continually inhabited metropolis in the world. The city's appearance, however, seemed to defy that fact. Here and there, one could see an ancient ruin, but each was surrounded by modern office buildings and wide, carefully landscaped streets. Flower gardens and tended lawns ringed the villas of the wealthy, giving the municipality its reputation as one of the most beautiful cities in the Middle East.

Damascus could be summed up in one simple legend: apparently, Mohammed himself had been reluctant to visit there because he desired to enter paradise only once.

Bolan parked the rented Escalade on the street and opened the driver's-side door. Father O'Melton got out on the other side, while Ahmad crawled from the backseat. Bolan waited, letting Ahmad lead the way down the narrow street. Above him, on both sides, Bolan saw *mashrabiyah* balconies, domed stone khans and mosque tombs. The streets were busy with foot traffic. Many of the men and women wore modern-day business attire. But others were clothed in traditional Arabic robes and headgear, and carried baskets containing everything from pastries to brass and iron items for sale.

"These are the streets the apostle Paul was led down as he contemplated his meeting with Christ on the Damascus Road," Father O'Melton said. Bolan glanced out of the corner of his eye at the priest and saw a lone tear sliding down his cheek. "I can't believe I'm finally seeing it."

The Executioner reached out and placed a hand on Ahmad's shoulder. "Hold on a minute," he said, turning him around. "It's time to regroup."

The three men stepped inside the entryway to a flower shop and dropped their voices to whispers.

"There's no way Father O'Melton or I can pass as Arabs," Bolan said. "So while you point out this café where Hezbollah meets, we'll need to stay far enough away that they don't see us with you."

"I understand," Ahmad said. "You have...what is it you call them? Bugs?"

"I've got a bug," Bolan answered. "It's actually a transmitter. It'll fit in your pocket and transmit any conversation back to Pat and me. But keep in mind that there'll be a short time delay before we understand what's being said. Father O'Melton speaks Arabic. I don't. French, Spanish, Russian and a few others yes, but Arabic, no." He stared down at the shorter man. He still didn't know if he could trust Ahmad, and that was something he could never let himself forget. The Arab's conversion to Christianity and willingness to turn against his former fellow-terrorists might be sincere. Then again, it might be a masquerade. So to be on the safe side, Bolan added, "We'll be recording the conversation, however. So we can play it back and pick up on any little nuances we might miss in real time."

The statement had been made to let Ahmad subtly know that he had not yet fully gained Bolan's trust. But if it bothered the former Hezbollah man, he didn't show it. He just nodded in understanding.

Bolan pulled the tiny transmitter from a pocket of his sport coat and handed it over. "Are they likely to search you?" he asked.

"I do not know," Ahmad said. "By now, they will know all about what happened at Saint Michael's Chapel. And they will be curious as to why I am the only survivor." He licked his lips nervously. "And, of course, word of my changing sides may have reached here. I suppose we are about to find out."

"We'll be as close as possible," Bolan said. "But it'll still take us a while to get to you if things go south. So keep that in mind—we can't guarantee you protection."

"I understand," Ahmad said.

"Still willing to go through with it?" Bolan asked.

Ahmad nodded.

"Well, then," Bolan said, turning the transmitter over to the former terrorist. "Put this thing somewhere they won't check."

Ahmad didn't hesitate. He stuffed the device into his underwear.

"You've got your story down, right?" Bolan asked. He, Ahmad and Father O'Melton had had plenty of time to come up with a cover story as Grimaldi flew them from the U.S. to Damascus in one of Stony Man Farm's Learjets. They had decided that the best cover was a partial truth: Ahmad was going to tell the Hezbollah at the café that he had pretended to convert to Christianity, and the priest had taken him out through a secret underground tunnel when the shooting started. He would stress that he had not *deserted* his comrades, but rather that the other Hezbollah members—those who had stayed in the chapel and died for the jihad—had all encouraged him to go.

They wanted at least one of their party to survive in order to report what had happened.

The story wasn't perfect. But it was the best they could come up with under the circumstances.

"Yes," Ahmad said reluctantly. "I have my story. Let us pray that they believe it."

"That'll all be up to you, Zaid," Bolan said. "And your attitude when you talk to them. You'll have to practically convince *yourself* it's the truth. You do that, and your sincerity will help convince them."

Ahmad nodded again.

Leaving the entryway, the three men walked on, reaching what for centuries had been known as the Street Called Straight. They made their way around other pedestrians coming toward them through the bazaarlike neighborhood, where old men in white turbans sat cross-legged in front of their shops. Bolts of striped *djellaba* and red calico were stacked and on sale everywhere. The three passed the House of Saint Ananias, and then the ruins of the Wall of Saint Paul, where, nearly two thousand years ago, the apostle had escaped persecution by being let down in a basket.

Finally, Ahmad stopped and turned to Bolan. "The coffee shop is two blocks from here," he said. "If you accompany me any farther, the men inside smoking hookah pipes and drinking sweet coffee will be able to see you through the glass front."

The Executioner nodded. "Okay, then." He reached into another pocket and switched on the receiver and attached recorder. "Go on. We'll monitor you. And Father O'Melton will translate as fast as he can. But remember—Arabic is a second language for him, so speak as slowly as you can without tipping them off. We should be able to tell a lot just by the tone of everyone's voices." He paused, staring down at the man again. "And we'll hear any gunshots."

Ahmad gulped, and it looked as if he were trying to swallow a softball. "If you hear gunshots, it will be too late to help me."

"That's right," Bolan said. He waited a moment, then intensified his stare. There were a lot of things Ahmad could do without broadcasting his betrayal over the transmitter, and Bolan wanted the man to know *he* knew it. The "converted" informant could even pull out the transmitter and silently show it to the Hezbollah terrorists. They would know something was going on without a word being said, and feed back misinformation.

Or come out of the café ready to kill Bolan and Father O'Melton.

"We'll be listening," Bolan finally said. "So don't mess up—on *either* end."

He could see in Ahmad's eyes that the man caught his meaning.

"Father O'Melton and I will find a place to sit down around here," Bolan told him. "Someplace where we'll look like ordinary tourists. Walk back down this street when you're done. We'll be somewhere where you can see us." He lifted a big fist and scratched his chin. "If you think you're being followed, ignore us and we'll ignore you. Just walk on past, and we'll meet outside the Omayyad Mosque in four hours. That should give you more than enough time to shake a tail without it looking like that's what you're doing."

Ahmad glanced down at the ground as if he might be saying goodbye forever. Then he nodded once more, turned and headed down the street.

The three men had passed a café a block earlier that had wrought-iron tables and chairs out front, beneath very European-looking umbrellas. Bolan turned that way and O'Melton followed. As they walked, Bolan pulled a tiny receiver out of his pocket and inserted it into his left ear. A second, identical earbud he handed to the priest.

The earpieces looked little different from those worn by many of the younger, Western-dressed Arabs who were listening to music on their iPods as they hurried along the crowded street.

"You suppose everyone'll think we're listening to Arabic rap?" Father O'Melton asked in a jovial tone as he inserted his receiver, then pulled out one of the wrought-iron chairs and sat down.

Bolan's answer was a simple smile as he dropped down across from the priest. A waiter appeared at their table, took the order for two cups of strong Arabic espresso, and disappeared again.

"Can you hear anything yet?" O'Melton asked.

"Just street noises," Bolan answered. "Our man hasn't reached the café." He stopped talking suddenly, then said, "Wait. He's there. Can you hear him?"

"Yeah," O'Melton said. "He's speaking to someone. Someone who's surprised to see him. It sounds like some of the other men there know him."

Bolan waited as he listened to half a dozen "Allahu Akbars" and similar greetings from the Hezbollah men. "I think he's sitting down now. If they're passing the hookah around they're probably on those big pillows."

"The Koran warns against the use of tobacco," O'Melton said.

"Not everyone practices what they preach," Bolan murmured.

"Amen to that." Father Melton frowned and stared down at the table in front of him. "Exactly what I was afraid of is happening. Ahmad's speaking fairly slowly. But the rest are talking so fast I'm missing some of it."

"This isn't going to work, then," Bolan said. "But I've got a backup plan. It wouldn't hurt to tune in a live feed to my base, where I have fluent Arabic-speakers. We can't afford any confusion or misinterpretation." Pulling his satellite phone from his pants pocket, he tapped in the number to Stony Man Farm. The waiter arrived with their coffee as the call connected, and Bolan heard Price say, "Yes, Striker?"

"Hold on a minute," he told her as the waiter set their cups and saucers on the wrought-iron table. When the man had left again, he said in a low voice, "Barb, I'm going to connect you directly into the bug I've got on our man inside a café. Father O'Melton is with me and speaks reasonably good Arabic. But they're talking fast, and there's always a chance of slang words or regional colloquialisms he might miss." Bolan paused to take in a deep breath. "So please tell me you've got someone there who speaks Arabic."

"Phoenix Force just got back from South America," the Stony Man mission controller said. "They've been three days straight without sleep and are upstairs in the bedrooms. But I can buzz Hawk."

"I'll hook the live feed in while you do that," Bolan said.

He connected the receiver to the satellite phone with a suction-cupped wire. A moment later, the chatter in Arabic was streaming straight from one satellite to the next and ending up at Stony Man Farm in the United States. Bolan had left the line open so he and Thomas Jackson Hawkins, the youngest member of the counterterrorist squad known as Phoenix Force, could converse back and forth.

A second later, the familiar Southern drawl came on the line. "I knew somebody'd make sure I didn't get any sleep," Hawkins said in a hoarse voice.

"You can sleep all you want when you're dead," Bolan said.

"And that could come any second," the man known as Hawk replied. "What have you got for me, Striker?"

"You have the phone to your ear?" Bolan asked.

"That's affirmative."

"Then listen to the Arabic in the background and see if you can interpret the important parts as we go. We're taping the conversation on this end, and Barb will be taping the whole thing there at Stony Man Farm, too. Later, you can go over it in more detail."

"Rumor here at the Farm has it you've got an Arabic-speaking priest with you," Hawk said.

"I do," Bolan said. "But he'll be the first to admit that while he can get along just fine in that language, there are nuances he very well might miss. Besides, two heads are better than one."

Both men fell silent as they listened to the stream of Arabic coming from the café. Then Hawkins said, "It sounds like several men can't quite figure out why one person isn't dead."

"That makes sense," Bolan said. "The man they're questioning is ours. The others are some of his former Hezbollah buddies. Does it seem like they're buying his story?"

"It's hard to say at this point," Hawkins replied. "There's a slight tone of skepticism. At this point, I'd say it's like betting on red or black at a roulette table. Maybe fifty-fifty."

"Don't forget the green 0 and 00," Bolan said.

"Yeah, well, he's feeding them a story about being in a Catholic chapel. Says he got out with the help of a priest when he pretended to convert to Christianity. They're all starting to laugh now."

"I can hear *that* on my own," Bolan said.

"They're making fun of the priest, and how gullible Christians in general are. 'They always believe what they want to believe' is almost a direct quote."

"What's your overall take, Hawk?" Bolan asked. "Is our man *really* our man or is he playing triple agent?"

"He's sounding like a Muslim," Hawkins said. "But that's what you wanted, isn't it? Hey, wait. Hold on a minute…."

Bolan and Hawkins quit talking, and the Executioner noted that the men speaking Arabic had lowered their voices. They were almost whispering.

The low, throaty sounds went on for perhaps a full minute. Then the voices returned to their normal tone.

"What was that all about?" Bolan asked.

"I'm not a hundred percent sure," the Phoenix Force operative said. "They were kind of talking in circles. The way men do when they're plotting something that needs to be kept secret."

"Anything more direct you can give me?"

"Well, your man—I've gotten to know his voice—seems to have gained their confidence. I guess they finally bought his story. Wait—" Thomas Jackson Hawkins's voice suddenly cut off as all three men tried to hear what was being said.

"I think I just heard the word *sarin*," Hawk said in almost a whisper.

Bolan looked across the table to O'Melton.

The priest nodded.

"Keep listening," Bolan said quickly.

A few minutes later, he himself recognized the "Allahu Akbars" and other expressions of goodbye, and then the sounds of the street outside the café.

Hawkins took a deep breath. "It looks like your man isn't burned. In fact, they've included him in an op they have planned for tomorrow night."

"You catch the details?" Bolan asked.

"Most of what you'll need, I think," Hawkins said. "We lucked out, because your snitch was a new face and had to have a lot of details explained that the other men would already know."

"So let's have them," Bolan said.

"Your guy is supposed to meet them back at the café tomorrow night around 2300 hours. They've got something cooking. Something big. Bigger than Saint Michael's, anyway. What *was* Saint Michael's, by the way? We've been in Argentina."

"Nothing you need to concern yourself about," Bolan said. "You've done a great job. Now, give me the rest."

"They've got sarin gas," Hawkins said. "And the name Saddam came up more than once."

"Saddam Hussein?" Bolan asked.

"That's what I took from the context," Hawkins agreed.

"But he's dead," Bolan said.

"I got the definite impression they—Hezbollah—have had the chemical weapons for a number of years. Or at least the Syrian government has."

"Then Saddam shipped the sarin out to Syria before the U.S. invaded," Bolan said. "And Syria is giving it to Hezbollah. If whatever strike they're planning comes off, Hezbollah takes the blame and the Syrian government pretends to know nothing about it."

"That was my take on the subject," Hawkins stated.

"Okay, kid," Bolan said. "You did a great job. "Now catch some Zs."

"One eye is already closed, Striker," Hawkins said, and hung up.

Down the street, Bolan saw Ahmad sauntering toward them, a grin on his face. He turned to O'Melton before the former Hezbollah man got within earshot. "Was that your take on things?" he asked the priest.

O'Melton nodded.

Bolan sat back in his chair and took a sip of his coffee. It had gone cold, but the caffeine would give him a jolt of energy. "Well, let's see how our friend's story stands up against what you and my man back home heard."

A moment later, Ahmad was at the table, saying, "Do you mind if we go inside? Who knows who might walk by and recognize me."

"I've got a better idea," Bolan said. He glanced down the street, toward a small hotel they had passed earlier. Aladdin's Lamp read the sign atop the three-story building. "You stay here for fifteen minutes," he told Ahmad. "Then come meet us in that hotel. I'll try to get a room on the top floor, facing the street. Don't ask for us at the front desk—who knows who you might be dealing with there? Just go down the halls look-ing at doors. We'll hang a jacket on the knob."

Ahmad nodded as he took a seat, glancing nervously around as if he suspected he might already have been seen.

Without further words, Bolan and O'Melton took off to-ward the hotel.

4

If he had to describe Aladdin's Lamp in one word, Father O'Melton would have said, "Dusty."

The former Army Ranger-turned-priest felt his sinuses swell and clog as he followed the man he knew as Matt Cooper up the ancient wooden staircase. Each step they took brought a creaking sound to the ancient wood. In the big man's hand, O'Melton could see the large key fob and the numbers 307 imprinted into the metal. In his mind, he registered the fact that the key holder could be used as a weapon—much like a yawara stick.

The thought caused the priest to laugh silently to himself. You could take a priest out of the Rangers, he concluded. But you couldn't take the Ranger out of a priest.

The room faced the street as they had requested, and O'Melton waited as the big man inserted the key into the door. The aged wood squealed as loudly as the stairs when the door swung open, and Cooper stepped to the side to let the priest in first. Then, with a quick glance up and down the hall to make sure no curious eyes were watching, he took off his sport coat and hung it on the knob before closing the door.

The room held a mixture of old and new furniture. To O'Melton, it looked as if the proprietors waited until one piece wore out completely, then replaced it with a more modern item. The bed frames—there were two of them—looked to be old, and the mattresses and box springs didn't fit. Both lapped over the sides of the wooden frames at least six inches, and sleeping—if they had time to sleep—would be a balancing act worthy of a circus high-wire performer.

A rickety wooden table against the wall at the foot of the beds looked as if it had come into the room about the same time. But the chairs around it were of steel, with cheap plastic making up the seats and backs.

Bolan moved to the end of the room, where a large dusty curtain covered the window. He pulled it back slightly, allowing a shaft of sunlight to drift in and highlight the dust motes that floated in the air and plugged O'Melton's sinuses. "I see you only travel first class," the priest said, breaking the silence that had fallen over them since they had checked into the hotel.

"Only the best for you, Padre," he said.

The priest laughed out loud and took a seat on the edge of one of the beds. Before either man could speak again, there was a knock at the door.

Bolan's guns—a Beretta 93-R and .44 Magnum Desert Eagle—had been exposed ever since he'd taken off his jacket. O'Melton watched as Bolan drew the Beretta from under his left arm and walked to the door. He raised the barrel of the automatic, covering the peephole for a few seconds, before lowering it and replacing it with his eye.

The movement was smooth and simple, but vitally important, O'Melton knew. It was a survival technique he'd been taught himself while in the Rangers. There was no better assurance of the enemy getting a head shot than seeing the inside of a peephole darken. A savvy assassin simply shot through the hole and into the eye. Much better to risk a little damage to a steel barrel first, to make sure whoever had knocked was one of the "good guys."

A moment later, Bolan opened the door and let Ahmad into the room.

The dark-skinned man took a seat on one of the steel chairs at the table as Bolan dropped into one directly across from him. Then, slowly and methodically, the big man began to question him in detail about the meeting at the café. Ahmad knew O'Melton spoke some Arabic. But the smaller man wasn't sure just how much, nor did he have any idea that they had hooked the transmitter feed to a satellite phone and streamed it all the way to America for another translation.

Bolan's questions were simple and friendly. But O'Melton knew he was testing the other man for any inconsistencies between what he said and what the man Cooper had called "Hawk" had translated earlier. Listening carefully, the priest noted that Ahmad's story fell pretty much in line with what the translator had told them. There were a few minor differences, but nothing beyond what would be expected about the same incident from another point of view.

If anything, the tiny inconsistencies confirmed the fact that Ahmad was telling the truth and that his "story" had not been rehearsed.

Finally, Bolan said, "Okay, Zaid. Make sure I've got this right as I sum it up. Hezbollah has chemical weapons—sarin gas, to be exact—which they secretly obtained from the Syrian government and which originally came from Iraq right before the U.S. invaded. They plan on moving the chemicals tomorrow night. The ultimate goal is to get them into the U.S., where they can be set free in an act of terror which'll make the World Trade Center look like a mere opening act. Am I right?"

"You are correct," Ahmad said.

Bolan pulled the satellite phone from his jacket and tapped in a number. As the airwaves began to connect, he said, "Then we've got tonight—and only tonight—to get to the sarin gas first. Do you know the location?"

O'Melton remembered the lowered voices during parts of the meeting they'd eavesdropped on. "Hawk" had been unable to pick it all up, and the priest suspected it was during this time that they'd spoken about specific details such as the location. It would have been human nature to do so.

"Yes," Ahmad said. "They are in the port at Latakia. I can lead you straight to them. But there will be guards."

"I expect there will be," the big man with the sat phone pressed to his ear said. The call must have connected at that moment because O'Melton saw their leader's eyes drop from Ahmad to the table in front of them. He quit speaking for a moment, then murmured, "Barb, I need Hal just as fast as you can get him." Then he became quiet again.

O'Melton waited patiently. He had no doubt that this big American operative had already worked out a plan in his mind. He had never seen an agent quite like Cooper before—not in the Rangers, and not even with Delta Force. Cooper was bigger, stronger, faster and smarter than any warrior the priest had ever met—and O'Melton had been a Ranger long enough to meet thousands of the "best of the best."

He shifted slightly, adjusting the featherweight Smith & Wesson .357 Magnum "Military and Police" revolver he still carried in its shoulder holster. He had added a Colt Special Combat Government Model to his personal arsenal. It was a handgun that he vastly preferred to the newer GI-issue Beretta 92, and the bags had contained the weapon in both .38 Super and .45 caliber versions. The .38 had been tempting—the magazine contained one more round than the .45. But the likelihood of finding more ammunition for what was primarily an IPSC—International Practical Shooting Confederation—competition round was low. So he had chosen the .45, and it currently rode on his right hip in a Concealex holster.

Other features—updated changes from the basic 1911 design that had served the U.S. for over a hundred years—were the rosewood-and-rubber composite grip slabs, white dot front Heinie dovetail and rear Bo-Mar sights. The skeletonized trigger was a nice touch, as well.

The priest shifted the hard plastic holster beneath his jacket. Its presence was beginning to irritate the skin beneath it. The same thing was happening with the double 10-round magazine carrier, which he'd attached to his belt on the opposite side.

While he readjusted the magazine caddie, Cooper began to speak. And the more O'Melton heard of the one-sided conversation, the more in awe he became not only of the man's prowess in the field of covert operations, but also the connections and "pull" he had to have in order to get all the things he began to request.

Father O'Melton sat quietly, listening to the big American and silently marveling at the fact that after several years as a retiring, mild-mannered priest, he was back in the same kind of action he'd performed while a U.S. Army Ranger. He didn't know exactly where this mission was headed. But of one thing he was certain.

He had no doubt in his mind that he was continuing to do what he was meant to.

BOLAN WAITED SILENTLY as the call bounced off the phony "trap" numbers and went from satellite to satellite before finally reaching Stony Man Farm. A moment later, he heard Price answer, and said, "Barb, I need Hal just as fast as you can get him."

It took only a few seconds for that to happen.

"Hello, big guy," the Stony Man director said. "What can I do for you?"

"A *lot*," Bolan said. "Here's the situation. We've got our

man back in with his old Hezbollah buddies and they appear to still trust him. We've also got the location of some twenty barrels of sarin, which are currently under guard at the port in Latakia. Now, here's the problem—Hezbollah is planning to move them out tomorrow night."

Brognola whistled on the other end. "That doesn't give us much time," he said.

"Do we have an aircraft carrier in the area?" Bolan asked.

"We're bound to have one somewhere in the Mediterranean," Brognola replied.

"Well, get a ship headed for Latakia," Bolan said. "But make sure they stay out in international waters. We don't want to tip our hand too quickly."

"I can make that happen with one phone call to the President," Brognola said. "What else are you going to need?"

"Helicopters," Bolan said. "The same stealth kind the SEALs used to take down Bin Laden. They need to be able to take on the cargo and they need to be on the aircraft carrier as soon as possible." He paused and glanced toward Father O'Melton. The priest was adjusting his new holster and magazine carrier, but listening intently at the same time. "Are Phoenix Force and Able Team there?" he said into the phone.

"Able Team is still busy on the Mexican border," Brognola said. "And I just sent Phoenix Force toward Australia. I can call them back—"

"No need," Bolan interrupted. "But get twenty blacksuits ready to jet toward the aircraft carrier." In his mind, he pictured the battle-hardened troops who were trained and stationed at Stony Man Farm. "Make sure they include enough pilots to fly the choppers."

"That," Brognola said, "I can do *without* a phone call."

Bolan paused and took a deep breath. "And make sure the blacksuits know what they'll be grabbing when they land."

"Do you know whether or not the sarin's been weaponized yet?" Brognola asked.

It was a good question—one that could mean the difference between life and death to the blacksuits and anyone else in the area when the strike went down this night. Bolan turned to Ahmad. "Has the sarin been weaponized yet?"

Ahmad looked confused. "What exactly do you mean?" he asked.

"In order to get maximum effect out of the gas, it's got to be mixed with binary agents. Do you know if that's been done yet?"

"No," Ahmad said. "I do not."

Bolan spoke into the phone again. "That's unclear at this time, but let's be on the safe side. Outfit all the blacksuits with Level A Demilitarization Protective Ensemble. And test each suit for heat sealing and air supply, as well as the escape air canister, communication system and heart-rate monitor."

"Ten-four," Brognola said. "I'll have Cowboy Kissinger on it as soon as we hang up. Do you want DPE suits brought in for you and your two men there?"

Bolan thought for a moment. If the sarin had already been mixed with the binary agent, a lone gunshot into one of the barrels would immediately contaminate the entire area. But even if the agent was still separate, a puncture would allow small amounts of sarin to leak out, which could affect anyone close by.

And that "anyone in the immediate area" included Father O'Melton, Ahmad and the Executioner.

"No," Bolan finally said. "There won't be time for us to suit up. We'll have already started taking out the guards by the time the first helicopter lands." He paused, knowing that the weight of O'Melton's and Ahmad's safety was falling directly upon his shoulders.

It was one thing to risk your own life. Quite another to risk that of some other, innocent person.

And endangering innocents was exactly what he was doing. At least with O'Melton. Ahmad's "innocence" still wasn't a hundred percent certain.

"We'll have to go in Level F," Bolan finally said. "Street clothes. But you can send along three gas masks for us just in case."

"Affirmative," Brognola said. "Anything else?"

"Yeah," Bolan said. "You know anybody over at NCEH?"

"The National Center for Environmental Health?"

"The very same. Know anybody?"

"Not that I can think of offhand," Brognola said. "But the President will."

"Then tell the President we want one of the top hands along to test for leaks. I assume he'll have his own Level A togs. You can pick him up in Washington with the blacksuits right before you fly this way, and you won't have to worry about him learning anything about the Farm." Bolan let a tiny smile curl his lips. Stony Man Farm was the most top-secret counterterrorist installation in the world. Even the CIA had no idea of its existence, and the military and law enforcement officers who were handpicked to train there were always brought in and out with blindfolds covering their eyes and the pilots pulling every "air show" trick in the book to keep them from knowing where they were until they'd landed.

It was Brognola who instigated the next subject of conversation. "You've still got Grimaldi there in Damascus," he said. "May I assume he'll be taking you to Latakia?"

"You may," Bolan said.

"Then I'll send the blacksuits and NCEH geek with Mott. He's been here ever since he dropped Able Team off."

Bolan thought of Charlie Mott. He wasn't quite the pilot Jack Grimaldi was, but he wasn't far behind. He'd probably use one of the Concords Stony Man Farm had purchased when the company went out of business, and he'd get the blacksuits to the aircraft carrier as fast as possible. "Okay then, Hal," Bolan said. "I guess that's all for now."

"Keep your phone on, Striker," Brognola said. "We're threading a needle here. This is going to take split-second timing."

"I know," Bolan said. A second later, he pushed the button to end the call.

Father O'Melton rose from his seat on the bed. "I take it that our stay here at Aladdin's Lamp is going to be a short one?" he asked.

"That's right," Bolan said. "We're heading to Latakia."

Bolan slid his sport coat over his weapons and started toward the door.

The other two men followed.

Latakia was Syria's primary Mediterranean port. A quiet city except for occasional political riots that spread there from Aleppo, it was famous for its tobacco crops. The streets were wider than those in most ancient Syrian cities and were lined not only with houses, but beautifully tended gardens and parks. Hilly pastureland surrounded the municipality, except for the side facing the rocky seashore. A Roman arch, reminding those who saw it of past conquerors, rose high in the sky, and the Mughrabi Mosque was famous for its panoramic view and the beautiful rugs on display.

None of which interested Bolan as Jack Grimaldi landed at the Latakia airport.

The Executioner's mind was on a thousand details of the strike they were about to make.

He had called ahead and reserved a Buick Enclave rental car. It required a minimum of paperwork, and a few minutes later Bolan, Father O'Melton and Ahmad were driving away from the airport toward the harbor area.

Night fell on the black vehicle as the smells of sea salt and fish began to penetrate the closed windows and doors. "You know the building where the stuff's stored, right?" Bolan asked Ahmad.

"Precisely," the allegedly former Hezbollah man said.

"There is a container terminal across from the quayside railway and next to the bridge."

"And enough room for the choppers to set down close by?" Bolan said.

"Yes," Ahmad replied. "Your men should not have to roll the drums more than thirty feet or so."

The harbor appeared in the distance and Bolan slowed the Enclave, falling in with other traffic on the road. They passed a floating crane, then the primary dock before Bolan pulled the vehicle in behind several large containers stacked next to the quay ramp. Pulling a set of night-vision binoculars from the console next to him, he raised them to his eyes. On the other side of the ramp, he could see a small storage building.

A man in green fatigues and a kaffiyeh stood outside the door.

In his hands was an AK-47.

"That the place?" Bolan asked Ahmad, handing him the binoculars.

The informant took a quick look and said, "Yes. In fact, I know the guard."

"How many other men are there likely to be?" Bolan asked.

"There is no way I can be certain," the man said. "But the chemical weapons are quite a prize. I would guess there are many."

Bolan lifted the satellite phone and tapped in the Stony Man Farm number. Price, the chief mission controller, would be handling the split-second timing necessary to make this strike a success, and it was she who answered.

"Yes, Striker?"

"We're on site," Bolan said. "One guard at the front door is all we see. But my man here is certain there'll be plenty more."

"Affirmative, Striker," she said in a cold, businesslike

voice. "The blacksuits are in choppers on the aircraft carrier, just waiting on you to give them the go."

"Okay, Barb," Bolan said. "We've got five helicopters, but there's no room around here to land more than one at a time. They need to come in three minutes apart. Each team will load four drums of the sarin and then take off. I want the next one right behind, ready to land. We'll be heading toward the building to take out the guards just as soon as I hang up."

"Gotcha, Striker. I'll get the first chopper started. Good luck."

"Striker out," Bolan said. He turned to Father O'Melton, who sat directly behind him. "Time to pass out the toys," he said.

O'Melton reached over the seat to the rear storage area of the vehicle and grabbed an M-16 A-2 assault rifle. He fished around for a moment before coming up with four extra 5.56 mm magazines, then handed the lot to Bolan.

Ahmad, who had sat in the front passenger's seat to guide Bolan, said, "Please give me one."

He shook his head. "If any of the Hezbollah men see you and get away, you're burned," he said. "You stay here in the car."

For a second, Ahmad's temper seemed to flare. "But I *want* to go," he said. "I *need* to go. I know you are not certain yet that you can trust me. And I want to prove to you that my conversion to Christianity and my desire to stop terrorism is sincere."

Bolan stared into the man's eyes for a long moment. Ahmad seemed sincere. But there were a lot of lives at stake here—not just the three of them in the Enclave, and the blacksuits, but all the men, women and children who would die if the sarin gas reached its target in the U.S.

And if Bolan's guess that Ahmad truly was on their side proved wrong, it would be easy enough for the Hezbollah man to shoot both him and Father O'Melton in the back during the gunfight that was sure to be coming.

On the other hand, proving he was sincere meant Bolan had one less worry to distract him as this mission went on.

Finally, Bolan glanced back at O'Melton and said, "Give him a rifle, Pat."

The priest did as instructed, then grabbed a third M-16 and extra magazines for himself.

The harbor was dark, save for streetlights scattered throughout the area. There were plenty of shadows between the Enclave and the guard in front of the door, but the quay ramp stood between them. And that presented a problem.

The ramp grew steeper the closer it got to the sea, and if they wanted to cross it while remaining out of sight, they'd have a ten-foot wall to pull themselves over before they reached the building. And it would be in darkness. But doing that with weapons would likely create noise, not to mention that they'd have to sling their rifles in order to use both hands, rendering them defenseless for several seconds.

And being helpless for no matter how short a period had never sat well with the Executioner. In this particular situation, if the guard at the door heard them, he'd be able to take all three of them out before they even got their rifles off their backs.

Bolan felt the muscles in his face tighten as he pondered the problem. The only other way to get to the storage building would be to cross at the top of the ramp. And that area was in full light, and plain view for the man in the green fatigues.

Bolan, O'Melton and Ahmad got out of the Enclave and quietly closed the doors. Bolan led the way to the steepest part of the ramp, then turned to the other two. Handing O'Melton his M-16, he whispered, "I've got to take that guard out quietly. Wait here. Don't come after me until he's down."

O'Melton and Ahmad nodded.

Moving quickly, Bolan drew the sound-suppressed Beretta from the shoulder rig beneath his sport coat. There had been no time to change into blacksuits, and he regretted that fact. He had his extra magazines stuffed into pants and coat pockets, and none were ideal for battle, let alone the gymnastics he was going to have to perform to get across the ramp.

Moving to the edge, Bolan dropped to a seated position, then pushed himself off into space. He landed on both feet, with a thud he knew sounded louder to him than it actually was.

The next part of his quiet assault was most critical. He had to get up and over the side of the ramp and put a bullet into the guard's brain stem before the man reacted. Once gunfire started, all the Hezbollah men around the chemical stash would be alerted.

Softly, in the distance, Bolan heard the sound of helicopter blades.

Walking quickly across the concrete ramp, Bolan stuffed the Beretta into the front of his pants, took a deep breath, then jumped upward, catching the top edge with both hands. A second later he had pulled himself up the other side and lay flat on his belly.

Looking straight into the barrel of the Hezbollah man's AK-47.

Bolan didn't hesitate. While the guard was still confused as to what was happening, he leaned to one side, drew the Beretta and sent a quiet 9 mm hollowpoint into his head. The man fell forward onto his rifle.

A second later, Bolan was on his feet and sprinting toward the prostrate body. What he found was a badly wounded terrorist. The bullet had been slightly off center, and the man was still breathing. He would die soon, but Bolan wanted him dead *now*. Even though the Beretta was suppressed, it wasn't silent, and the Executioner didn't want to risk even the quiet *pfffffft* it would make this close to the building.

So, pulling the Spyderco Navaja from his pants pocket, he flipped open the blade, knelt and drew the razor-sharp edge across the man's throat. A gusher of blood—like a just-tapped oil well—blew from the side of his neck.

Bolan wiped the Navaja's blade on the dead man's BDU shirt, then turned toward his teammates. They had dropped down into the ramp themselves, and handed up their rifles. He took them, laid them down, then helped pull O'Melton, then Ahmad up and over the side.

The pulsing of blades from the first chopper was getting louder, which meant it was time for Bolan and the other two men to take out the rest of the guards. Pointing O'Melton toward the right side of the building, he waved him that way. As the priest took off running, the Executioner directed Ahmad ahead of him to the left.

The building wasn't particularly large, and the two men reached the corner in less than twenty steps. Bolan had run to the side and just behind Ahmad, keeping one eye on him as they went. As soon as they rounded the corner, they saw two more men in green fatigues standing guard at a side door. Both had lit cigarettes in their mouths, and the orange tips gleamed in the shadows.

Bolan raised his M-16 A-2 and flipped the selector to semi-auto. He sent a lone round just to the side of one orange glow, and watched the bullet obliterate the terrorist's face. A half second later, Ahmad proved he could operate an M-16, drilling his own round into the belly of the other guard.

Bolan continued running, and was almost on top of the gut-shot man when he pulled the trigger again. His round hit slightly higher, and the 5.56 mm hollowpoint splintered both itself and the terrorist's heart.

Bolan and Ahmad continued sprinting down the side of

the building, passing windows that had been painted over in black, then turning the corner to the rear of the structure. They could hear O'Melton firing full auto at whoever he had encountered on the other side.

Only one man stood behind the building, and there was no rear door. He lifted his AK-47 as Bolan and Ahmad appeared, but the Executioner was a half second ahead of him. Pulling the trigger twice, he sent a pair of 5.56 mm rounds into the terrorist's chest not two inches apart.

Bolan would not be around for the autopsy, but didn't doubt that whoever performed it would have a hard time finding any pieces of the man's heart.

Running footsteps sounded, approaching the far corner, and Bolan turned his attention that way. Raising his rifle once more, he fingered the trigger, then released it when Father O'Melton appeared.

At the front of the building, Bolan could hear the first helicopter landing. He paused for a moment, thinking. They needed to enter the building, where the WMDs were stored. But they had no protection whatsoever.

And one tiny round piercing a fifty-five gallon drum might be enough to kill him, Ahmad and O'Melton. Yet the longer they waited, the more time any men inside would have to prepare for what was obviously an assault on the storage site.

Bolan took a deep breath, considering exactly where they stood. The men in the chopper would have brought them gas masks, as instructed. The masks should protect them from the deadly agent alone. But if the binary was in place—and a drum was pierced—they'd still die.

Should they go on in without the masks, doing their best to avoid hitting the sarin containers, and hope the Hezbollah inside didn't just start shooting into the drums as their own personal and unprompted "suicide bomb"? Or take the time to go back around the building and put on their masks first?

The question had come to the Executioner in a heartbeat, and he made his decision just as fast. "Go to the chopper!" he ordered Ahmad and O'Melton. "Get your masks on, then Pat takes the side he came down. Zaid, take the other side."

"And you?" Ahmad asked as all three men started running back around the building.

"I'm going in," Bolan said, as he sprinted on ahead.

"Without your mask?" Ahmad asked.

Bolan didn't answer; he just kept running. When he finally caught sight of the chopper, he saw that five Stony Man Farm blacksuits had already disembarked and were making their way toward the concrete storage building. In their Level A, single-use positive pressure suits they had an otherworldly appearance. Like astronauts walking on the moon, or something out of *Star Wars*.

Bolan's first thought was that the suits, while protecting them, would hinder their agility and speed. They were likely to be cut down in the doorway when they tried to go in after the big, heavy drums. And as sure as he knew his own name, Bolan realized it was up to him and his own men to lead the way.

At the same time, he saw that his decision to enter the building maskless while he sent the other two men after breathing protection would not be necessary.

The Level A man in the lead held an M-16 in his right hand as he approached the front door. From his left hung three gas masks. Bolan let his own rifle fall to the end of the sling as he ripped one of the masks out of the man's hand and pulled it over his face. "You wait until the gunfire dies down," he said. "*Then* come in."

The gas mask facing him nodded vigorously.

Bolan had already started toward the front door as O'Melton and Ahmad donned their own masks. There was no time to wait. The men inside—and Bolan knew there had to be some in there—would be over the shock their sudden attack would have prompted, and would have had time to think.

Which was dangerous. The more time they had to consider, the sooner the thought of just drilling the sarin containers full of holes might cross their minds.

Bolan reached the front door, grasped the knob and found it locked. *More* time for the men inside to prepare their defenses or begin shooting the drums, he thought as he stepped back and riddled the lock area with 5.56 mm rounds. The door popped slightly open, and Bolan grabbed the knob again, swinging it wide. He went in low, and felt a dozen enemy rounds buzz over his head and back as he entered.

There was no cover. Not that he'd have any time to take it if there had been.

Bolan saw the sarin drums in the middle of the one-room building, standing upright in rows and painted yellow. Above them, he saw a loft of sorts that ran completely around the storage area. And perched around the railing were at least a dozen more Hezbollah men dressed in green BDUs and aiming their AK-47s down at him.

Bolan's first instinct was to begin shooting. But at the same time, he realized that if there were men in front of him and to the sides, there had to be some directly behind and above him, too.

And the unseen men posed the most danger at the moment.

Diving to the ground as the 7.62 autofire came toward him, Bolan hit the concrete in a shoulder roll, twisting to face his rear as he came up on one knee. He had switched the M-16 to 3-round burst, and his first trio of semijacketed hollowpoint rounds took out a man wearing a turban above his "greenies." The guard flipped over the rail and landed three feet in front of the Executioner.

Bolan swung his rifle to the right, drilling three more 5.56 mm slugs into the chest and throat of a bearded Hezbollah man above and slightly to the side. In his peripheral vision, he saw that two more were trying to get him in their sights, and he rolled again, just before a dozen or so AK-47 rounds hit the floor where he'd just been. Sparks flew through the air like Fourth of July sparklers as the bullets bounced off the concrete, and Bolan could only hope that none were hitting the yellow drums.

With another pair of 3-round bursts he took out the two men firing at him. Only one Hezbollah guard still stood at the railing above him now, and Bolan noted that the man had redirected his fire to the side of the building.

Which could only mean that O'Melton had entered the side door and joined the fray.

Directing a final burst into the man's chest, Bolan watched him fall back from the rail, then turned in the direction he had been shooting. Sure enough, O'Melton had made it inside and was firing his own American battle rifle up at the men in the loft. As he lifted his M-16 again, Bolan saw a kaffiyeh-wearing figure catch three of the priest's rounds and fall over the rail, landing on top of the yellow drums.

Bolan glanced quickly at the barrels, wondering if any of them had been punctured. But he didn't belabor the point. If they had been, he, O'Melton and Ahmad would know it soon enough.

And it might very well be the *last* thing they ever knew on this earth.

A long-haired man with an even longer beard suddenly switched his point of aim to the other side of the building, telling Bolan that Ahmad had joined the fight, too. The beard flopped up and down beneath the man's chin as he cut loose with a steady stream of fire from an Israeli Uzi.

The irony of a Jew-hating terrorist being more than willing to use a weapon invented and manufactured by Israelis wasn't lost on Bolan. But this was hardly the time to philosophize about such inconsistencies, and the big American sent a trio of rounds through the beard and into the man's upper chest and neck.

The Uzi fell from the loft, clanking and bouncing against the yellow barrels before finally settling on top of them. The man himself slumped headfirst over the rail, hanging upside down, with blood dripping from his wounds.

Bolan felt the vibration as several rounds hit the concrete floor next to where he lay, and he rolled away, spotting the shooter upside down while in the middle of the roll. As soon as he landed on his stomach, the soldier fired a final two rounds from his weapon, and then the bolt locked open on an empty magazine.

There was no time to switch them out, so Bolan rolled slightly to his side and drew the Desert Eagle from his hip. Raising it in front of him, he tapped the trigger and a lone .44 Magnum hollowpoint slug caught the shooter squarely between the eyes.

The top of the man's head blew off as cleanly as if he'd been scalped.

Bolan fired again, catching a Hezbollah man in the chest with a double-tap of rounds. From the corner of his eye he saw Ahmad down another man wearing a turban, and then suddenly the building went quiet.

The only sounds as the blasts of bullets died down were the ringing in the Executioner's ears and the heavy breathing of Ahmad and Father O'Melton.

Bolan jumped to his feet. "Pat," he called out as he started for the front door. "Keep guard. We don't want any supposedly 'dead bodies' coming back to life and killing us."

The former Army Ranger saluted.

"Let's go," Bolan said.

He ran through the door to where the first Level A–

outfitted blacksuit stood, rifle ready. The others had gathered just behind him.

"Where's the guy from NCEH?" Bolan said.

One of the Level A men stepped from behind the leader. Unlike the other men, he bore no rifle. But his arms were filled with a variety of equipment Bolan didn't even try to identify.

He pointed toward the door. "Get in there and find out where we stand," he said. "And be quick about it. We've still got to load this stuff and get out of here before the Syrian regular army shows up."

"Are you sure the Syrians will be coming?" the dressed-out NCEH man asked.

Ahmad had appeared through the doorway in time to hear the question, and it made him laugh out loud. "Of course they will be coming," he said. "It would be impossible for Hezbollah to have used this storage facility without the government's knowledge." He paused and drew in a deep breath.

"Which makes them enemy combatants," Bolan said simply. Still looking at the NCEH man, he added, "Now get going."

The agent nodded, ducked slightly and hurried into the building. Ahmad looked up at Bolan. "All the Hezbollah inside are dead," he told him. "Father O'Melton and I checked each one individually."

As he spoke, O'Melton exited the building, as well. As soon as he was outside, the priest reached up and took off his gas mask. "The guy inside said it's safe to take these things off," he said. "None of the drums were even punctured." An unusual smile—as if he knew something the others didn't—lit his face.

Ahmad shook his head in awe. "With all those rounds being fired," he muttered. "And not even *one* of them hit the containers. The odds against it must be phenomenal. We are truly lucky."

As all the blacksuits sprinted in to begin transferring sarin gas to the helicopter, Ahmad and Bolan took off their masks. "Luck had nothing to do with it, my young convert," the priest said. "*Never* underestimate the power of prayer."

While Bolan, O'Melton and Ahmad watched, helping here and there when needed, the blacksuits from the first helicopter loaded their drums into the chopper and took off.

Almost immediately, the second aircraft landed, and five more men from Stony Man Farm sprinted out to do their duty, rolling more drums of chemical agents onto the stealth helicopter.

Bolan glanced at his watch. They were making decent time. But it was still a lengthy and nerve-racking process. And he knew that Syrian soldiers and/or police would show up any second.

All the choppers needed to be gone before that happened. And if possible, he, O'Melton and Ahmad had to disappear from the scene, as well.

As the final helicopter landed and began loading sarin, Bolan heard the sound of sirens over the whirl of the rotor blades. They were still a ways off, but would arrive soon. The assault on the sarin storage site, the battle both inside and out, and then landing each chopper and loading the yellow drums had been loud and long. Somebody—probably a lot of somebodies—could have called in.

When the last chopper had secured its load of drums, the blacksuit pilot looked to the Executioner and saluted. As he did, Bolan saw the first of a long line of Syrian personnel carriers squeal around a distant corner and head toward them.

Uniformed men hung out both sides of the vehicle, aiming AK-47s their way.

More trucks turned behind the one in the lead. Bolan quit

counting when he reached an even dozen. Pausing for a second, he did some quick mental calculations. Even if each vehicle carried only ten armed Syrian regulars, that amounted to one hundred twenty troops who would soon be upon them. He, O'Melton and Ahmad could stay and fight if they wanted. But they'd eventually be mowed down like wheat beneath a combine.

Bolan knew there was a time to fight.

He also knew there were times for tactical retreats, so you could live to fight another day.

And this was one of those times.

"Get on board the chopper," he shouted to O'Melton and Ahmad as the first shots from the AK-47s began flying past them. "And you," he said to the saluting pilot, "get this thing off the ground and out of here."

Bolan helped shove O'Melton and then Ahmad up into the cargo area as the helicopter lifted off. Two rounds shot past him—one in front of his face, the other just behind his head—and he felt the heat of both burn him like a sudden sunburn.

The odor of his own singed hair filled his nostrils.

The helicopter had begun to rise as Bolan let the M-16 A-2 fall to the end of its sling, then jumped up to catch the skid a split second before it rose out of reach. As bullets continued to fly from the weapons of the Syrian regulars, he pulled himself up and over the skid, finally taking a hand from O'Melton, inside the helicopter.

A few seconds later, the state-of-the-art stealth chopper had risen out of effective range from the small arms on the ground.

Bolan stood up inside the chopper and eyed the blacksuits crowded around the yellow fifty-five-gallon drums. No one seemed to have been injured.

"Thanks for the lift," he told O'Melton. "You're pretty strong for a priest," he added with a smirk.

Father O'Melton just laughed out loud.

The conversation stopped there as they flew to join the other stealth helicopters on the U.S. Navy aircraft carrier offshore in international waters.

6

A three-quarter moon had played peekaboo with the clouds ever since the final helicopter had taken off from the sarin storage site, and Bolan had watched the waters below go from small, white-tipped waves to total blackness and back again each time the glowing orb passed behind a cloud.

The aircraft carrier was roughly fifteen miles out from Syria, safely in international waters. It should have made for a short flight. And it did.

It just didn't seem that way to Bolan as he contemplated his next move in this intricately complex mission to protect the world from the weapons of mass destruction that the former Iraqi dictator had "farmed out" to sympathetic countries.

As he held on to an overhead strap, Bolan suddenly sensed a presence next to him. Turning, he looked down slightly to meet the eyes of Father O'Melton. The former Army Ranger was checking both his featherweight Smith & Wesson M&P .357 Magnum and the Special Combat Government Model .45 ACP to make sure they were ready to go.

Bolan had watched the priest do the same thing just prior to their attack on the storage building, with the .45, .357 and his M-16 A-2. It was a time-honored exercise performed by many warriors the world over. It served not only the obvious purpose—to make certain their weapons were good to go—

but also as a way to keep their minds occupied both before and after battle.

It helped keep the "creepies" from crawling into a man's brain and soul.

When he had replaced both weapons in their holsters, O'Melton looked up at Bolan. "I've got this picture that keeps running through my mind," he said. "I see this dog chasing a car down the street. Then, suddenly, the car just stops. And the dog looks around in bewilderment because now that he's caught the car, he doesn't know what he's supposed to do with it."

Bolan had heard the comparison before. What O'Melton was really trying to say was now that we've got the sarin, what do we do with it?

"These drums aren't our problem anymore," Bolan said. "We turn them over to the folks on the aircraft carrier and they take them to a disposal site."

"Where's that?" the former Ranger asked. "And exactly how do they dispose of them?"

Bolan shook his head slowly. "We're getting out of my field of expertise now," he said, as the moon came out from behind a cloud and the whitecaps appeared blow again. "But it's my understanding they go to one of several locations in the U.S. One's at Pueblo, Colorado. There's another one in Lexington, Kentucky, and a few more around the country that I can't remember right now." The moon hid behind another cloud, darkening the sea below them once more. "But my guess is that since these drums will already be on board a ship, they'll be heading for Johnston Island."

"Johnston Island?" O'Melton said with a frown on his face. "Never heard of it."

"It's a small atoll about eight hundred miles west-southwest of Hawaii, in the central Pacific," Bolan said. "It's the safest disposal site. If something goes wrong, the sarin gas has a lot of ocean to cross before it gets to any major populations, and it has time to dissipate before it arrives."

O'Melton was looking into the darkness as the moon crept back out again and illuminated his face. "Okay," he said. "But do you know how they dispose of it?"

"Again," Bolan said, "this is outside my frame of reference. It's the kind of thing I leave up to the guys with the thick eyeglasses and white lab coats. But they tell me they incinerate it."

"Incinerate it?" The priest turned to face him once more. "I'd think that would poison—"

"The air with sarin-soaked smoke," Bolan finished for him. "I know. But, for whatever their reasons, the lab rats seem to have found burning it all up to be the safest way possible of getting rid of it." He paused and drew in a deep breath. "They were just storing and guarding these things for a while. But that always left open the possibility that they'd fall into the wrong hands again."

Both Bolan and O'Melton fell silent, and the only sounds were the overhead chopper blades and the wind rushing past them as they flew on to meet the aircraft carrier. Bolan lowered his eyebrows in concentration as he contemplated the next leg of the mission. A quick glance back into the chopper showed him the shadowy form of Ahmad sitting crosslegged on the deck, slightly apart from the blacksuits, who were still crowded around the yellow drums.

Bolan knew that he had been lucky to get Ahmad for this op in Syria. The man not only spoke fluent Arabic, with his Hezbollah links he had been able to obtain direct intel on where the sarin had been stored. And he had continued to prove that his conversion to Christianity through Father O'Melton was sincere, and not just some ploy that Hezbollah had come up with.

The Executioner frowned more deeply. Unless, of course,

Ahmad's actions were all part of a larger "master plan" beyond the scope of Bolan's current thinking. He had watched
the man mow down his former Hezbollah brothers with his
M-16, and under most conditions, that would have been proof
enough of the man's loyalties. But Bolan had to remind himself that Hezbollah, like other radical terrorist organizations,
used suicide bombers on a regular basis.

What if Ahmad had killed his comrades in what was just
another form of "suicide" sacrifice to further the jihad? What
if he was masquerading as a Christian in order to set up some
bigger strike against the Western world, and the men he'd
killed had allowed him to take their lives so they could go
straight to paradise?

It was not yet the time to take his eyes completely off
Ahmad. And Bolan had begun wondering if that time would
ever come.

The sound of the overhead blades changed, and Bolan
looked back out the chopper door to see the lights of the
huge aircraft carrier below. Two choppers were still in the
air and ready to land before them. They would have to wait,
and the Executioner's mind went back to the next phase of
the mission.

The former Iraqi dictator had farmed his chemical weapons
out to Syria—that was a fact. But CIA, NSA and Stony Man
Farm intel had all come up with the knowledge that the Iraqi
butcher had also developed biological and possibly at least
one short-range nuke. So where were *these* WMDs? Also in
Syria? That was possible, but Bolan's gut told him that the
dictator would never have trusted any of the surrounding
countries with *all* the "aces up his sleeve." During the period
in which the U.S. was obviously planning to invade Iraq, the
dictator would have firmly believed he could hide out until the
Americans went home again, then be restored to his throne.

He'd have had no idea that he'd be caught, tried by the World Court, and end his life dangling from the end of a rope.

So he likely would have been skeptical of giving any other Arabic countries too many of his secret WMDs. He would not have wanted the balance of power in the Middle East to change when he returned to lead Iraq once more.

The first of the two stealth helicopters set down on the aircraft carrier as the moon came back out to add illumination to the ship's lights. So where, Bolan wondered, had the bioweapons and nuke gone? Afghanistan? Not likely—U.S. troops were already in control there and likely to intercept any smuggling attempts. Pakistan? Equally unlikely, but for different reasons. Pakistan had been playing both sides against the middle since their neighbor had been invaded after the 9/11 attacks in New York and Washington, D.C. Could these nightmarish weapons have gone to Yemen? That was a distinct possibility. The small nation just below Saudi Arabia on the map had been known to harbor terrorists.

And then there was Iran. Even though Iraq and Iran had fought a long and bitter war back in the twentieth century, they might well have merged together in their joint hatred of America.

After all, Bolan thought as the second helicopter landed below his, there was an old saying that fit this situation perfectly: *the enemy of my enemy is my friend.*

But how was he to know which country or countries had taken on the remaining WMDs? And even if he could ID the nations in league with the fallen dictator, how was he to start? In Syria, he'd had a former Hezbollah man for a snitch.

In these other Arabic countries, he had no one.

As the last chopper ahead of them landed on the aircraft carrier, the satellite phone in his breast pocket began to vibrate. Pulling it out, he glanced at the small screen and saw the letters *SMF*. It was Stony Man Farm calling. Most likely Barbara Price.

"Striker," Bolan said as he punched the button with his thumb. "What's up, Barb?"

"I just got a call from Grimaldi," she said. "He tells me the mission went well and that all the drums are on board the aircraft carrier."

"They will be as soon as we land this last chopper," Bolan said. He paused a moment, then added, "How did Jack know that?"

"Because he's waiting for you on the ship below, in one of the Learjets," Price said. "All fueled up and ready to go."

"You obviously know something I don't," Bolan said. "Go where?"

"Tehran," Price said. "Kurtzman and his team have been monitoring the chatter on the internet. We've been able to decipher and translate a lot of it." The beautiful honey-blonde mission controller paused for a second and drew in a breath. "At least enough to know that Iraq's biological warfare supply and research laboratories were transferred to Iran."

Bolan didn't answer for a moment as his mind took in the new intel. Finally, he said, "We have anybody on the ground there?" he asked.

"There's a former CIA informant who might know something."

"The operative words in that sentence are *former* and *might,* Barb," he murmured. "Why is the guy *former?*"

"We don't know for sure," she said. "Kurtzman hacked into the Company's files, but they didn't say anything about why the man was terminated."

"Great," Bolan answered. He turned away from where Ahmad still sat, and lowered his voice so the former Hezbollah man couldn't hear him. "Just what I needed. Another snitch I'm not sure I can trust."

"Well," Price said, "he's all we've got at the moment. Kurtzman and the rest of the gang will keep on listening and hacking away. In the meantime, you want to go in or not?"

"Of course I want to go in," Bolan stated. "It's like you said. If it's all we've got, it's all we've got."

"Affirmative, then," Price replied. "I'll advise Hal, and he'll brief you once you're on the plane with Grimaldi. In the meantime, good luck."

7

They were going in cold, with no immediate contact to guide them.

In undercover circles, that was considered the best way to get burned.

And probably killed.

Bolan's boots hit the ground in the small clearing among the trees a little harder than he'd expected, and he rolled onto his left shoulder, spreading the impact throughout his body, before popping back up onto his feet. He glanced upward just in time to see Ahmad land similarly, then his eyes moved on to Father O'Melton.

The former Army Ranger hadn't been quite so lucky. His parachute had snagged in the scrubby limbs of a leafless tree, and he presently swung back and forth ten feet above the ground.

Since the man was in no immediate danger, Bolan hauled his chute in, folded it and moved back out of sight into the trees. He scraped a shallow hole in the dirt with an entrenching tool and dropped the parachute into it. He was about to cover it with a large boulder when Ahmad appeared.

Laying the former Hezbollah man's canopy on top of his own, Bolan left the boulder where it was and turned back to O'Melton, who was still swinging in the air, muttering unintelligible words that Bolan doubted he had learned in the seminary. But as he watched, the commando-turned-priest pulled a slim black object from his pocket. A second later, a loud click echoed through the still clearing and Bolan saw the distinctive blade of a Columbia River Knife and Tool Hissatsu folding knife in his hand.

The Hissatsu was a unique blade, in Bolan's estimation. Strong, wickedly sharp, and the most fast and powerful of the many folders currently sporting assisted openings, which worked much like switchblades. But they got around the law by not utilizing either a push button or latch opener. Instead, the knife wielder began opening it by pushing out on the disc near the top of the blade. When the steel was roughly thirty percent exposed, the spring kicked in and snapped it the rest of the way out.

A moment later the Hissatsu had severed the shoulder straps of both the parachute and the priest's large backpack, and he'd dropped to the ground, landing on his feet in a squatting position.

The Hissatsu, Bolan knew, had come from one of the storage lockers mounted in the rear of Grimaldi's Learjet. All aircraft flying out of Stony Man Farm were kept packed with gear that might be needed during an operation. In addition to O'Melton adding the assisted-opening folder to his personal arsenal, all three men had replenished their ammunition supplies during the flight.

Bolan left the trees and walked up to O'Melton as he disengaged the top lock and closed the blade again. Like Bolan and Ahmad, he was outfitted in a blacksuit, and he clipped the Hissatsu back into the zippered pocket he'd retrieved it from.

"Nice job," Bolan said. "Only a couple of problems as I see it."

"And they are…?" O'Melton let the sentence drift in the air.

"First," Bolan said, "your chute is waving in the breeze

like a formal announcement that we're here. Second, we can't walk around Tehran in these blacksuits. You're going to need the clothes that are still hanging up there in your backpack."

"Then it looks like Shinny City," the priest said. Without further words, he wrapped his thighs around the trunk of the tree, shinnied up to the first limb, then climbed up two more to where his chute and oversize backpack hung.

The CRKT Hissatsu reappeared and the chute and pack fell to the ground.

The priest descended to the lowest limb, then jumped the rest of the way. Tucking his own chute on top of Bolan's and Ahmad's, he helped the Executioner roll the boulder over to cover the evidence of their arrival.

A moment later, all three men were changing into light-weight business suits, transferring their armaments as they did so.

"Are you sure we should not wear traditional Muslim dress?" Ahmad said as he thrust a 9 mm Tokarav pistol into the holster on his belt before donning his coat.

"It might work for *you*," Bolan said. "But for Father O'Melton and myself it would not be so easy. Our faces would give us away in a split second."

Ahmad shook his head. "Actually, it is not unusual to see some Iranians with fair skin and blue eyes."

Bolan sat on the ground, pulling off his jump boots and trading them for rubber-soled hiking shoes. As he laced them up, he said, "Not unusual, no. But not the norm, either. So we need to play the odds. We don't want to stand out any more than we have to." Leaving the top button of his light white cotton shirt undone, he transferred the Desert Eagle to his belt holster and slid on the shoulder rig for the Beretta 93-R. Extra magazines for the Beretta hung under his left arm, and those holding more .44 Magnums went into the caddie on his belt just behind the big Eagle. Clipping the Spyderco Navaja into his waistband, he stood up and donned his jacket.

The North American Arms .22 Magnum Pug minigun went into the hip pocket of his pants, held in place by a pocket holster that also carried an extra five rounds of the hollow-point ammo.

From the corner of his eye, Bolan had watched Father O'Melton change into his own off-white business suit. He still wore the blackened S&W Scandium .357 revolver in the same shoulder holster he'd had on when Bolan first met him. His .45 he had simply stuck into his belt amid a series of .38/.357 speed loaders and .45 magazines held in place by ballistic nylon pouches.

All three men pulled briefcases from their extra-large backpacks, then used the same entrenching tool to dig another hole to secrete the packs next to their chutes. Inside the packs, in addition to other equipment they might or might not need, were the traditional robes and headdresses of Islamic mujahideen that Ahmad had inquired about. Bolan wanted them handy just in case they did prove useful down the line.

No one knew what curves a mission such as this might throw at you.

The Executioner only knew that the curves would *come*.

Dropping the folding shovel on top of the pile, he rolled another stone over the hole to cover it. Then he walked around the area, scuffing his feet to obliterate any tracks.

Finally, he knelt and unlatched the briefcase he'd pulled from his backpack. Opening the lid, he lifted out a Heckler & Koch MP-5 submachine gun. Checking to make sure a round was chambered from the 30-round stick magazine, he looked up at Ahmad and O'Melton. "We're locked and loaded," he said. "You ready?"

The priest had been checking his own weapon. "I'm good,"

he said. Turning to his new convert, he asked, "You ready, Zaid?"

Ahmad had pulled the bolt on his MP-5 all the way back, causing the chambered 9 mm round in the barrel to pop out. "Whoops," he said softly, then disengaged the magazine and started to replace the round at the top.

Bolan reached out and grabbed the weapon from the former Hezbollah terrorist's hand. "You never do that," he said.

"Do what?" Ahmad's eyebrows drew together in mild confusion.

"Put a round that's already been cycled back into the magazine." Bolan tugged the MP-5's bolt back again and ejected the new round. "When it goes into the chamber, a round gets 'nicked.' And that nick—if it gets hung up on the loading ramp or the ejector—can cause a jam." He took the round and tossed it into the trees. "You've got twenty-nine left," he said. "Go with that to be safe. Besides, you've got extra 30-round mags in your briefcase."

Ahmad nodded. Bolan stood up and walked to the edge of the trees. They had jumped from Grimaldi's Learjet using a HALO—High Altitude Low Opening—technique, and landed just where they'd wanted to—in the middle of a clearing atop a small hill just outside Tehran. They were halfway between the capital city and the village of Rey. And from where he stood, Bolan could see both communities below.

"I never did quite catch on to what we're supposed to do next," O'Melton said.

Bolan paused a moment. Compared to their strike in Syria, they were truly going in blind. The only advantage they had was that just before they'd jumped, word had come down from Stony Man Farm that Kurtzman had located, and established contact with, the one-time CIA informant.

Details weren't yet available, but it appeared the man in question had severed ties with the CIA rather than the other way around. It seemed that he believed he'd been double-crossed by his handlers, and left hanging out to dry in the last operation he'd assisted them with.

The Executioner also learned that at first contact with Kurtzman, the informant wanted no part of the mission Bolan was currently conducting.

Aaron "the Bear" Kurtzman, however, was not only a computer genius, but also a master of diplomacy. During the time Bolan and his sidekicks had been on the aircraft carrier, and then on the jet headed toward Iran, the wheelchair-bound man had convinced the ex-informant that he would *not* be working with the CIA. And the offer of an even million dollars for his help hadn't hurt Kurtzman's argument, either. Particularly when five hundred thousand dollars had suddenly appeared in a Cayman Island bank account assigned to the Iranian, with a promise to pay the other half million upon completion of the mission.

"We've got to get down this hill to the road," Bolan said as soon as all three men had changed and were ready to move. "We'll be picked up by a guy named Ali Mohammed."

"We will look strange, coming out of this forest wearing these clothes and carrying briefcases," Ahmad said.

"Yeah," Bolan agreed, "we will. But not as strange as leaving these woods wearing blacksuits and carrying assault weapons." He paused a moment, then added, "I don't know a better way to get this thing started. If you do, I'm willing to listen to it."

It had been a rhetorical question. And Bolan got no response.

"Okay then, let's get this part over with as fast as we can," Bolan said. He led the way out from the clearing, through the scrubby trees and down the hill. He did feel a little on the conspicuous side. While much of the current Iranian population dressed in robes, turbans and other traditional cloth-

ing, many others had returned to the Western dress that had
become typical during the reign of the Shah. Even the Iranian president was most often seen wearing a business suit
with an open collar.

Bolan and the other two had patterned their attire after
him.

As soon as they reached the roadside, Bolan felt better
about their appearance. Kurtzman had arranged for Ali Mohammed to leave an old Dodge Ram van on the shoulder,
with steam shooting up out of the open hood from the ra-
diator. In a few seconds they went from wrongly dressed
men in the woods to what looked like a trio of businessmen
or salesmen whose vehicle had broken down along the road
leading into Tehran.

"When's this guy supposed to show up?" O'Melton asked
as Bolan lifted the hood of the Dodge.

"Any time now," he replied. He was tempted to take off
his jacket and roll up his sleeves to make it look as if he
was trying to fix the problem with the engine. But doing so
would have revealed his weapons, and he didn't like the idea
of taking them off and hiding them in his discarded coat or
under the car.

Five minutes went by. Then ten. And as they waited, several automobiles zipped past without a pause. O'Melton and
he were obviously foreigners, and the Iranian government
didn't encourage helping infidels in any way.

Finally, Bolan realized that they had been there long
enough that continuing to wear his coat had become conspicuous. Anyone who had broken down along the road would
be trying to fix their vehicle. At least one of them needed to
look as if he was trying to figure out what the problem was.
So after a quick glance up and down the road to make sure
there were no prying eyes, Bolan shrugged out of his jacket
and shoulder rig, then slid the Desert Eagle holster and other

equipment off his belt before rebuckling it. Wrapping the pistols and extra magazines in his jacket, he laid them carefully on the ground, just under the Dodge's front bumper. He had just finished rolling up his sleeves when another car passed by.

As Bolan fiddled aimlessly under the hood, the next car miraculously pulled over onto the shoulder. Loaded with a family of what appeared to be a father and mother in the front seat, and three curious children in the back, they offered their help. They were obviously not the former CIA snitch with whom Kurtzman had communicated, and both Ahmad and O'Melton—who spoke Farsi—convinced the family of would-be rescuers that help was already on the way.

The second group to stop was not so altruistic.

The two men in the front seat of the aged Plymouth, and the duo in the back, were dressed in flowing white robes and more colorful outer garments. All four stepped out of the car as soon as they'd parked directly in front of the Dodge.

Bolan didn't speak Farsi. But he didn't need to. Even before the men had uttered a word, he sensed that they were Persian bandits who thought they'd fallen upon a trio of helpless foreigners, whose vehicle undoubtedly contained items of value just waiting to be plundered.

"*Salaam,*" Ahmad and O'Melton both said. But Bolan could tell by the tone of their voices that they had sensed the danger, too.

The four road bandits didn't answer as they walked slowly and ominously back toward the Dodge. Bolan thought briefly of the Beretta and Desert Eagle concealed in his jacket, just below his feet. If the men from the Plymouth were armed— and they most likely would be—he'd be dead a hundred times over before he had time to unwrap his own weapons.

As if his thoughts were a self-predicting prophesy, the bandit in the lead suddenly drew a wickedly curved Arabian *jambiya* blade from beneath his robe. Two of the other men did the same—one coming up with a Persian *Pesh-kabz* and the other a flamboyant *shamshir* sword boasting a gold-inlaid steel hilt, whose long, curved kris-style blade he had somehow managed to hide inside his clothing.

The fourth man was far more modern. A Heckler & Koch 45/USP semiautomatic pistol suddenly appeared in his hand.

The Executioner didn't hesitate. None of these men were Ali Mohammed.

And none planned to leave him, Father O'Melton or Ahmad alive after they'd plundered their vehicle.

In one swift motion, Bolan drew the North American Arms .22 Magnum Pug and thumbed back the single-action hammer. The man with the H&K was the last in line as the bandits came toward him. But the pistol meant he represented the greatest threat.

So the first .22 Magnum hollowpoint from the Pug went squarely between his eyes, just above his nose.

The gunman dropped his pistol to the ground. His body followed a second later.

The robed man with the *Pesh-kabz* was just in front of the pistolero, and he turned, scrambling for the fallen gun. While he was busy doing that, Bolan swung his minigun toward the man in the lead—the bandit with the *shamshir*. As the soldier cocked the little .22 Magnum once more, the swordsman sent a deadly slash toward the side of his neck, hoping to sever his head from his body.

And had he been a tenth of a second faster, he would have accomplished just that.

But Bolan's battle instincts were in high gear, and he sensed the blow coming before it had even started. Ducking low beneath the blade, he felt it pass over his head—actually cutting off a small portion of the hair on the back of his head as it passed by. Knowing that a return slash would follow, Bolan wasted no time, aiming the minigun up from his crouched position and sending his second .22 Magnum slug into the right eye socket of the *shamshir*-wielding bandit.

The man who had the *Pesh-kabz* retrieved the Heckler & Koch from his fallen comrade and snapped off a wild shot in Bolan's direction. It missed him by a good five feet. But as he raised the minigun once more, he saw the bandit grasp the German-made pistol with both hands and take better aim.

Bolan's third round from the five-shot minigun struck the side of the bandit's face, tearing through his cheek and shattering the jawbone before exiting out of the back of the neck. It caused him to drop the H&K slightly, but did no permanent damage. Bolan's fourth .22 round, however, angled up into the bandit's open mouth and into the brain, causing an immediate shutdown of both small and large motor skills.

The handgun fell to the ground for the second time. And yet another body followed it.

The bandit who had drawn the *jambiya* was almost on Bolan, the thick blade of the edged weapon pointed straight at the big American's heart and about to thrust. Bolan's final shot hit the man in the chest, causing him to flinch.

But he continued forward.

Bolan knew the small caliber bullet would be bouncing around inside his attacker's chest cavity. It had been a death shot.

But he also knew one other vital bit of information. Although .22s were often deadly—and .22 Magnums even more so—they rarely killed quick enough to immediately shut down a determined attack.

The man Bolan had just shot would die. But he had a lot of time left to use the *jambiya* before that death overtook him.

Out of ammunition and with no time to reload or go for the guns wrapped in his jacket, Bolan dropped the minigun and jerked out the Spyderco Navaja. With a flip of his wrist, the 3.75" blade appeared in his hand.

The *jambiya* began thrusting toward him with the last of the bandit's breath and strength. Bolan stepped slightly to the side, out of the center line, and tapped the hand holding the blade away from him.

The Spyderco went straight into the bandit's throat, and when he felt it stop at the hilt, Bolan slashed in the direction of the edge. A fire hose spray of crimson shot forth from the robed man's neck as Bolan pushed him even farther to the side to avoid the blood.

It had taken only a matter of seconds. All four of the Iranian road bandits lay dead on the ground.

Bolan turned back toward Ahmad and O'Melton. Both had drawn weapons, but neither had had time to join in the battle.

"I was a Ranger a long time," O'Melton said in awe. "But I've never seen anything quite like that in my life."

Ahmad's mouth hung open, conveying basically the same message.

"Help me get these Cretins out of sight and back into their car," Bolan said without further ado.

One by one, they dragged the dead bodies back to the Plymouth and piled them into the front and back seats.

A moment later, a Toyota Highlander pulled to the side of the road.

Only one man was inside the vehicle, and this time, it was the right one.

Ali Mohammed.

8

Situated on a plateau in the northeast of Iran, the Elburz Mountains create a scenic view from Tehran, with the cone-shaped Mount Damavand rising higher than the other peaks. The panorama hadn't changed in thousands of years.

But the view was practically the only thing that didn't change in Iran.

In the days of the Shah, Iran had become a westernized country somewhat similar to Israel. As a friend of the U.S., it had enjoyed a booming economy and progressive attitude. Iranian military personnel, especially pilots, had been trained in the United States, and even undertaken joint practice operations with American forces. But the Shah had overstepped his power, using his infamous secret police—the Savak—to become a deadly dictator. And eventually, as always happens sooner or later in such cases, the people of Iran had revolted.

In what seemed like the twinkling of an eye, the Shah had been forced to flee to the U.S., and an exiled Muslim clergyman, the Ayatollah Khomeini, had taken the seat of power. Khomeini had then turned the country into an even more repressive, backward, Islamic theocracy.

But many years after the Ayatollah's death, another movement was simmering within Iran. Students in particular were tired of the archaic philosophies forced upon them. And while they had not yet gained the power it would take to return Iran

to a democracy, the country was once again split in its attitude toward a government based upon sharia law.

The mountains were clearly visible as Ali Mohammed
guided the Toyota Highlander the last few miles through the
outskirts of Tehran. He and the three men with him had rid-
den in near silence since disposing of the bodies of the road
bandits and entering the vehicle. But Bolan knew it was time
to talk. To find out just exactly how this new informant was
capable of helping them.

Not to mention beginning to form an opinion as to whether
or not the Iranian could be trusted.

Bolan rode in the shotgun seat of the Highlander, with
Ahmad directly behind him and Father O'Melton behind the
driver. They had retrieved the backpacks that had fallen with
them from the sky, and stored them in the rear of the vehicle,
and Bolan had returned his primary weapons to their hiding
places beneath his jacket.

As the only sounds within the car were those that managed to penetrate the rolled up windows, Bolan turned to
Mohammed. "Tell me why you ended your relationship with
the CIA," he said.

The man wore a white turban with a gold crescent moon
holding it together in the center of his forehead, but was otherwise clad in an off-white business suit and maroon necktie. He continued to stare at the road ahead as he answered,
"I was double-crossed." Venom seemed to drip out with the
words. "And it nearly cost me my life."

Bolan sat quietly for a moment, thinking. He had worked
with the CIA many times in the past, and it was certainly
not beyond them to expose their informants if they believed
it would serve a higher good. But the relationships and work
done by both "Company" handlers and their indigenous
agents on the ground were extremely complex, and misun-
derstandings were frequent. So, as much to simply satisfy his

own curiosity as to build on the shaky trust that currently existed between Mohammed and his team, Bolan said, "Someone burned you?"

"Yes," he said through clenched teeth as he drove on.

"Who?" Bolan asked. "Your handler?"

"It is impossible to be sure," Mohammed said. Manipulating the steering wheel with his left hand, he punched in the cigarette lighter on the dash with his right, then fished through his suit jacket, coming up with a crumpled package of Turkish cigarettes. By the time he had stuck one in his mouth, the lighter had popped back out, ready.

As the man in the driver's seat of the Highlander lit his cigarette, Bolan said, "You realize we aren't connected in any way to the CIA, don't you?"

Mohammed took in a deep lungful of the strong smoke, then spoke as it drifted back out of his mouth. "I know that is what you *say*. And I know that is what I have been told." He paused and the smoke stream finally ended. "Whether I believe it or not remains to be seen."

"Funny," Bolan said in a deadpan voice. "That's exactly the way I feel about *you*." He turned slightly in his seat to face Mohammed. "Whether you're actually trying to help us or are leading us into a trap…at this point, I don't know. So I guess we both need to trust each other as much as we can until we've proved our intentions beyond a reasonable doubt."

"That is the way I see it," Mohammed said.

"Tell me something," O'Melton said, leaning forward in the backseat. "Exactly when did your relationship with the CIA get exposed?"

Mohammed glanced over his shoulder at the priest, then returned his eyes to the road. They were entering the city proper, and the traffic was becoming thicker. "A few months ago," he finally said. "I do not remember the exact date."

O'Melton glanced at Bolan, then turned his attention back

to Mohammed. "That was about the time all the Wikileak stuff started coming out," he said. "You remember—that guy who hacked into U.S. government secret files, then posted it all on Wikipedia?" He continued to lean forward, his head almost over the seat. "It's quite possible that that's how you got burned—that the CIA had nothing to do with your exposure."

"I have considered that possibility," the man said, and Bolan thought he noticed a slight change of tone in his voice. It was as if the Iranian CIA informant *wanted* to believe his exposure had been a mistake rather than an intentional sacrifice by the "Spooks," but could never be sure.

In any case, it left room for doubt. And that doubt provided about as much trust as he, O'Melton and Ahmad were likely to get. At least until opportunities to prove their common interests presented themselves.

Bolan took a deep breath and the acrid smoke of the Turkish tobacco filled his sinuses.

"Well, tell me, then," he said, as the Highlander was forced to slow even more in the thick traffic of central Tehran. "If you don't trust us, how come you're doing this in the first place?"

Mohammed laughed out loud. "For the oldest reason in the world," he said simply. "The money. A million dollars will allow me to leave this Allah-forsaken country and its seventh-century attitude and government, and live the rest of my days somewhere in peace."

Bolan decided to play devil's advocate. "The money won't do you much good if you're dead," he said. "If you don't think you can trust the CIA anymore, what makes you think you can trust *any* Americans?"

The man in the driver's seat slammed on the brakes as another vehicle cut in front of him. He leaned on the horn, then extended his right arm into the air, his fist pointed toward the ceiling of the Highlander, and slapped his biceps with his other hand. It was the equivalent of giving someone "the finger."

"I am not sure I *can* trust any Americans," he said as traffic came to a stop. Outside the car, Bolan could hear the racing of engines and an occasional string of Farsi that sounded very much like curses. "But a million dollars will make a man take chances he would otherwise pass by."

Bolan nodded. It made sense. "So," he said, as they waited in the stalled mass of cars, trucks, bicycles and other vehicles. "Once you were burned, how come the Iranian government—or the al Qaeda cells they sponsor—didn't kill you?"

Mohammed was dragging so deeply on his cigarette that is was already halfway down to the butt. "Do not ask me how," he said. "But I talked my way out of it. They believed me."

Bolan sat silent again for a moment. That didn't seem very likely. Simply denying such allegations wouldn't make hardcore terrorists accept him again after being told he was a CIA snitch.

"I don't think words alone would do the trick," he said. "They would have wanted proof that you were on their side. And such proof would have demanded *action*."

For a brief moment, Mohammed's dark brown skin turned a grayish hue. He swallowed hard, his throat looking like a python devouring a chicken. Finally, he said, "I performed some *actions,* as you say. Actions which proved I sided with Islam instead of America and Israel. I had no choice. If I had refused, I would have been killed."

Once again, Bolan sat silently, thinking. In the backseat, he could hear the breathing of O'Melton and Ahmad. The traffic sounds outside the Highlander continued to penetrate the windows and doors, but seemed distant, and somehow added to the loneliness inside the vehicle.

Bolan knew that these "actions" Mohammed spoke of meant strikes against the United States, Israel, or more likely, both nations. He was sitting in the Highlander next to a man who had committed terrorist acts against Bolan's own country. Of course they had been undertaken in order to save Mohammed's life. But they doubtlessly had taken the lives of innocent American military personnel or citizens—or both.

Could Bolan, in good conscience, work with such a man?

He stared at Mohammed's face, noting the thick hairy eyebrows and long brown-and-gray beard. He reminded himself that you didn't get informants off Sunday school class rolls. In order to know what was going on inside a criminal or terrorist organization, a man had to have been part of that organization. A good snitch—*any* good snitch—had undoubtedly committed acts for which he should be imprisoned or executed.

That was what made such a man effective.

The bottom line, once Bolan had thought things through, was simple. He could not change the past; there was no way to go back and undo the despicable acts for which Mohammed was undoubtedly responsible. But Bolan *did* have a certain amount of control over the present and future of his informant and the two men working with him. So he would take things from there. And while he reminded himself that he still needed to keep an eye on both Mohammed and Ahmad, he would use them as much as he could to complete this portion of the mission at hand.

In any case, it was time to change the subject. "What can you tell us about the weapons of mass destruction Iraq palmed off into Iran before the U.S. invaded Baghdad?"

The confused mass of vehicles forming the traffic jam they were in began to move slowly forward as Mohammed said, "They are biological weapons. Not chemical like the dictator used on his own Kurdish people, and the Iranians during their war."

"Do you know what kind of bioweapons we're talking about?" Bolan asked.

"As best I know, they are smallpox and anthrax cultures," Mohammed said.

"Do you know where they're being stored?" Bolan said.

"No," Mohammed replied. "I don't even know if they are in the hands of the Iranian government or al Qaeda."

"But you can find out…?" Bolan prompted.

"I believe so. Given enough time to make it appear I am not directly searching for their location."

"Time is something we don't have," Bolan said. "We need to find these things, and we need to find them fast. Before they can be unleashed." He paused and drew in a breath. "Compared to the chemical weapons we got in Syria, the bio-cultures are small and easy to smuggle just about any place in the world. Meaning America, England, Israel or any other free nation." He paused once more, then stated, "You're not a rookie at things like this, Ali. Where does your gut tell you they are?"

"My guess—and it is only a guess, if an educated one—is that they would be stored somewhere in one of the science buildings at the University of Tehran."

"And why do you say that?" Bolan asked.

"Because they would have the facilities for climate and other controls," he said as the traffic gradually began to speed up. "These are somewhat perishable items. And they would need frequent care."

"Then you think the government, rather than al Qaeda, has control of these cultures?"

Mohammed glanced at Bolan. "It is often hard to distinguish between the Iranian government and al Qaeda these days," he said. "This is why I want out of my country. Why I am willing to risk my life to obtain enough money to do so."

"So," Bolan said. "You have a plan to locate these bio-weapons?"

"A plan, yes. Not a particularly good one, but a plan none-theless."

"And it is…?"

"I have a friend in the biology department at Tehran University. He may know. If he doesn't, he may know someone who does. As you might guess, rumors about all of this have run rampant."

While he didn't voice the words, Bolan had to agree with Mohammed. It wasn't a *good* plan by any means. And rumors were often as much of a hindrance as they were a help. If Bolan wasn't careful, he could spend months tracking down false leads. Months he, and the Western world, didn't have.

But at least he had a place to start. And if this was all he had, then it would have to do for the time being.

"Can you take me to meet with your friend?" Bolan asked.

Mohammed snorted through his nose. "Only if I want both of us to be killed," he said. "You do not speak Farsi. And you look about as Iranian as one of your own Alaskan Eskimos."

It was pretty much the answer Bolan had expected. "How about him?" he said, hooking a thumb over the seat to indicate Father O'Melton.

Mohammed tapped the accelerator a little harder as the jammed traffic began to speed up again. "Does he speak the language?" he asked.

"Yes," Bolan said.

"Let me hear him then."

O'Melton leaned forward in his seat again. *"Esfahan nesfe jahan,"* he said.

Mohammed let out a short laugh, then turned to Bolan. "He has chosen an ancient adage from the days when the city of Esfahan was one of the largest stops on the trade route from east to west and back again. It means 'Esfahan is the center of the world.'"

Bolan waited as a short silence fell over the vehicle. He could tell by the inflection in the Iranian's voice that more was coming.

"His accent, however, would give him away in a second. It sounds like a cross between American and Irish. And his face is the same, and confirms the fact that he's a foreigner."

Another hush fell over the slow-moving Highlander. Finally, as traffic came to a halt once more, Mohammed turned and looked at Ahmad. "Him, I could take," he said. "He would fit right in with little to no explanation needed. I do not like dealing with Arabs—"

"And I do not like dealing with Persians," Ahmad interrupted, verbalizing the ancient animosity between the two races and cultures.

"—but I will when I must," Mohammed finished, then shot a dirty look over his shoulder at Ahmad.

Bolan could tell the two men were going to become *great* friends.

But he didn't comment right away. He didn't care if the two men liked each other, only that they worked together to help him find the WMDs. He sat back in his seat and closed his eyes momentarily. He had not had time to test Mohammed's loyalty, and still was not completely convinced that Ahmad had truly had a change of heart. So did he want them taking off together—even if they didn't appear to be able to stand one another—and engaging in a vital part of this mission, without his supervision? He didn't know. If he assumed Ahmad could be trusted, then the former Hezbollah terrorist would monitor Mohammed's actions. But if Ahmad was just setting him and O'Melton up for some "big fall," allowing him to pair up out of sight with Mohammed could be disastrous.

After all, the two men were both Muslims. And that religious bond might be stronger than their cultural hatred for each other.

To complicate matters even further, Bolan didn't want either man to be aware that he didn't trust them. So if he refused to let them work together on this, he would have to phrase his words carefully, in a way that didn't give away his suspicions.

Finally, he opened his eyes and turned back to the man driving the Highlander. "I think you should make contact with your friend at the university alone," he said. "It's going to take a certain amount of delicate diplomacy to engage his help without giving away the fact that you're actually working for us. And any new face—no matter how Persian-looking or how well its owner speaks Farsi—is going to create at least a small amount of suspicion." He paused to let his words sink in, then said, "And you'll already be creating too much suspicion just by asking this guy where the bioweapons are stored."

"Then I will meet with my friend alone," Mohammed said. "As is your wish. I, too, believe it is better to work things that way."

Bolan studied the man's profile, looking for any signs of deception. Sending him in alone brought with it its own dangerous possibilities. Mohammed had already received half his million-dollar reward for helping them. It was safe and secure in an offshore bank account. So there was always the chance that he would decide five hundred thousand dollars was enough, and turn on Bolan and his associates before it became obvious to the Iranians and al Qaeda that he was an informant.

There was much to be said for settling on half the money, and leaving no anger in the hearts of his enemies, which might induce them to instigate a worldwide manhunt for him.

But the Executioner had found, in many missions over his long career of fighting evil, that there were always calculated risks that had to be taken. You controlled every part of an operation you could, but at some points you had to let loose the reins and hope for the best.

And this was one of those times.

"I take it you're heading for the university now," Bolan said.

"I am."

"How much longer?"

"Ten minutes," Mohammed said. "Perhaps twenty. It depends on the traffic."

"Where are we supposed to be while you go talk to your friend?" Bolan asked.

"You can just stay in the car," Mohammed said. "You will cause no excitement that way." He glanced at Bolan, his eyes running from the top of the big American's head down to his hiking shoes. "There will be many students, and even faculty, dressed as you are."

Bolan nodded silently. Then his battle instincts took over, and he knew that within the next hour or so he would know where the smallpox and anthrax cultures had been hidden.

Or else he, O'Melton, Ahmad and possibly Mohammed, would be dead.

9

"According to my friend," Mohammed said, as soon as he'd crossed the parking lot to where the Highlander hid amid a sea of other vehicles, "the most likely place for the biocultures to be hidden is not here at the main university." He had stuck his head inside the open driver's side window as he spoke.

"Get in," Bolan ordered. "We don't need to let every student on campus know what we're up to."

Mohammed opened the door and slid in behind the wheel as young men and women, some dressed in traditional attire and others wearing more Western clothing, passed by the Highlander on their way to and from classes.

As soon as the Iranian had settled into his seat, Bolan said, "Then where are they?"

"My friend has heard rumors that they are next door—at the school of medical science."

Bolan sat quietly, taking in this new information. Tehran University and the Tehran University of Medical Sciences, had separate administrations, but shared the same campus. Which meant the anthrax and smallpox cultures were somewhere right in front of them. Where, exactly, had yet to be determined. They might be hidden anyplace within the many divisions of a school of medicine. Finding them wouldn't be like finding a needle in a haystack, but more like finding a specific needle in a great stack of identical ones.

"Can you narrow it down a little more?" Bolan suggested. "We can't exactly go from room to room searching the whole medical school."

"My friend—" Mohammed started to say.

"Let's give your friend a name, shall we?" he interrupted. "I've got a feeling you, or all of us, are going to need to talk to him again, so we might as well treat him as a genuine entity."

"His name is Ajib Hasan," the man said. "And while he does not know exactly where the cultures are hidden, he has noticed a heavy military guard, both day and night, around the Traditional Pharmacy Research Center."

Bolan sat silently for a moment. Then he said, "Did he seem suspicious of your questions?"

"Not particularly," Mohammed said. "He has close ties to al Qaeda himself. And I—even though it is erroneous, of course, and part of my cover—am known to be aligned with them, too." He held a fist to his mouth and coughed. "It all came off like two old friends who had not seen each other in some time, discussing a mutual secret which they shared."

"And this military guard," Bolan said. "It's unusual on the medical school campus?"

"No," Mohammed said. "There are always soldiers roaming both campuses—especially at night. They are like your American security guards. But Ajib says some are permanently stationed at the Pharmacy Center. *That* is somewhat unusual."

"How big is the building?" Bolan asked.

"Big," Mohammed said simply.

The Executioner shook his head. They were going to have to enter the place and find the biological WMDs. If they took out the guards, no matter how quietly, on their way in, other military men roaming the campus were likely to notice. And they would clamp down on the Pharmacy Research Center immediately.

He and his followers were likely to be trapped inside even before they found the smallpox and anthrax.

Which meant Bolan and his men had to get in, find what he was looking for, and get out again—fast. If they took out the guards upon leaving, it would not be so bad. They could still escape with the cultures they'd come for before an organized resistance could be formed.

But how were they to actually find the deadly viruses once they were inside? Bolan neither spoke nor read Farsi. O'Melton, Ahmad and Mohammed did—but none of the men had the expertise to look through the various cultures bound to be stored inside, and determine which ones were weaponized and dangerous.

An idea hit Bolan as he contemplated the problem. "Is Ajib familiar with smallpox and anthrax?" he asked Mohammed.

The man nodded. "It is not his specific field of expertise. But as a biologist, he should have a working knowledge of such things. More so than the rest of us, at least."

"Then you need to go back and invite Ajib to dinner tonight," Bolan said. "We're going to have to take him with us when we go in."

A look of fear suddenly fell over Mohammed's face. "But if I do that, he will know I am working with you," the Persian said. "Al Qaeda, or the government, will kill me."

"That's where your million dollars comes in," Bolan said. "You're getting paid, and paid well, to take risks like that." He paused a moment, watching the man's face. "I'll do my best to get you out of the country as soon as we get what we're after. Then, with all of that money, a big wide world opens up to you."

Mohammed shook his head almost violently. "This is Iran," he said. "One of the least free countries in the world. You cannot guarantee my safe passage out of harm's way."

"I can't *guarantee* that any of us will get out of here alive," Bolan agreed.

"I cannot do this," Mohammed said, almost in tears.

"Yes, you can," Bolan said. "You don't have any choice."

"I can refuse."

"Yes, I suppose you could." Bolan stared directly into the man's dark brown eyes. Then swiftly and smoothly, he drew the big Desert Eagle from his Concealex holster and shoved the muzzle under Mohammed's nose, pressing it hard against the skin covering his top row of teeth. "And I can just pull the trigger right now and end all of your worries forever," he said in a low, menacing voice.

Mohammed was struck speechless. His eyes crossed almost comically as he stared down at the barrel of the big .44 Magnum.

Bolan had made his point. He holstered the Desert Eagle once again. "Or," he said in a slightly friendlier tone, "I can go into those biology offices, find your friend Ajib and let him know you're working with us right now. Actually, I'd kidnap him first and make him help us find the viruses. But then I'd tell him all about your past work for the CIA and how you led us to him."

Mohammed had begun to calm a little since the gun had been removed from his face. But suddenly his anxiety returned in spades. "You cannot do that!" he almost screamed. "That would be murder!"

"Not in my book it wouldn't," Bolan said. "You've got a past history with al Qaeda. Which means before you went to work for the CIA, you were responsible for the deaths of who knows how many innocent men, women and children. That's what made you valuable to the CIA, and now to us. But it also makes setting you up to be killed a matter of justice rather than murder." He stopped talking long enough to draw in a deep breath. "So get back in there and tell Ajib to meet you here in this parking lot at seven o'clock tonight. Tell him whatever story you need to in order to get him here."

Mohammed's face had turned permanently gray. "What is to keep me from just walking into the building and out the other door?" he asked.

"The fact that I'll burn you good if you do," Bolan said. "You might get away from us now. But if you don't return, I'll make sure word gets out about your CIA connection. Do you really want both the Iranian government and al Qaeda after your head while you try to escape Iran on your own and get to your half million?"

"You are completely ruthless," Mohammed said bitterly

"Only when I have to be," Bolan retorted. "And considering the things you were involved in before you rolled over to the CIA, what I'd be doing seems like mere child's play."

Mohammed opened his mouth to speak again, but closed it just as fast. Without another word, he got out of the High-lander and disappeared into the same building he'd been in earlier.

Bolan, O'Melton and Ahmad sat waiting.

"Do you think he'll be coming back?" Father O'Melton asked.

"I do," Bolan said. "He doesn't really have a choice."

Fifteen minutes later, Mohammed came back out of the same door he'd gone in. He walked swiftly to the vehicle and got behind the wheel. "Ajib will be here at seven-thirty," he said. "He has a staff meeting until then."

Bolan nodded. "Does he suspect anything?"

"I do not believe so," the Persian said. He was looking down at the floor of the vehicle. But then his eyes rose to meet Bolan's. "And afterward, you will do your best to make sure I get out of Iran safely? And collect the rest of my payment?"

"Sure," Bolan said. "Assuming we all don't get killed first."

AJIB HASAN WAS AS PUNCTUAL as he'd promised to be.

The luminous green hands on Bolan's chronograph read exactly 7:30—1930 hours, to his military thinking—when the man approached the Highlander. He was half inside the vehicle on the passenger's side before he even noticed the three men crammed into the backseat.

"Ali, what—" he got out between his lips before Bolan raised the mammoth Desert Eagle .44 Magnum and motioned the al Qaeda contact on in.

As soon as the door closed and the dome light was extinguished, Bolan leaned forward. "You're going to go on a little adventure with us tonight, Ajib," he whispered, so softly it sounded terrifying.

"Ali, what is happening?" Hasan finally got the whole sentence out of his mouth.

The former CIA contact shrugged dramatically, his shoulders rising to his ears before dropping once more. "Things have changed since we last saw each other," he said. "You will do exactly what this man tells you to do. Or we will both die."

A moment of courage obviously overtook Hasan, who turned around in his seat and rose to his knees. "I will do *nothing* for you, infidel!" he snarled. Then his eyes dropped to the .44 Magnum, and Bolan sensed what was about to happen.

Hasan suddenly brought his hands together in a classic disarm maneuver—one taught all over the world and designed to break the opponent's trigger finger against the guard as the gun was snatched away. He performed it perfectly, even twisting his body sideways in order to diminish it as a target, while his arms moved.

It would have worked beautifully on most gunmen.

But Bolan was *not* most gunmen.

And when Hasan's hands slapped together, the barrel of the .44 Magnum was no longer where it had been a split second before.

Bolan had drawn the Desert Eagle back and away from
the man, and it stopped just to the side of his pectoral muscle.
Without pause, he thrust it forward, almost as if throwing a
spear. The end of the barrel struck the al Qaeda–sympathizing
professor just above his nose.

The Persian man screamed at the top of his lungs.

Bolan reached up, grabbed the man's hair with his left hand
and jerked him down over the back of his seat. For the first
time, he noticed that Hasan had recently had hair transplants,
and the top of his head looked very much like carefully cul-
tivated rows of stalks in some Nebraska farmer's cornfield.
Bolan glanced quickly out through the windows of the vehicle, front and back, left and right. None of the students drift-
ing back and forth from the parking lot to the buildings had
been close enough to hear Hasan's scream, or see the brief
tussle inside the Highlander.

Bolan held on to Hasan's hair, shoving the barrel of the
Desert Eagle up under the man's chin. "That was your free
one," he said. "But you only get one. You try to take this
away from me again and I'll turn your head into scrambled
eggs." He swung his gaze toward Mohammed. "Drive," he
said simply.

Hasan looked almost comical, turned around on his knees,
with Bolan holding his throat down against the top of the seat.
By this point, many of his hair plugs had come loose, some
falling over the man's face and ears. With the Desert Eagle
still under his chin, Hasan stared cross-eyed at the barrel as
they left the parking lot.

Bolan had no need to give Mohammed directions. During the time between his afternoon visit to the university and
while they waited for Hasan's arrival that evening, they had
scouted the area for a good place to interrogate the al Qaeda
contact. Mohammed drove a somewhat confusing route of

both left and right turns as he headed for the spot Bolan had finally decided upon.

"Where…where are we going?" Hasan asked in a trembling voice.

"I believe I told you to shut up," Bolan said, jamming the barrel of the big Desert Eagle a bit harder against the loose flesh beneath Hasan's chin. "I'll tell you when it's time for you to talk. And then you'll talk plenty. Or else you'll die."

But it had not just been finding an interrogation location that had occupied Bolan's brain during this interval. He had also been plotting exactly what strategy he could follow to get him and the other men into the Traditional Pharmacy Research Center without alerting the military guard. The first thought to come into his mind had been a clandestine full blacksuit entry. But with the exception of former Army Ranger O'Melton, none of the others were experienced in such black op maneuvers. And if they were spotted during their approach, or after retrieving the WMD cultures—and that was almost a certainty, considering the fact that the men had no idea what they were doing—there would be no explaining their garb, weaponry, or the other equipment carried openly on their persons.

Another possibility was a clandestine entry in the street clothes they all wore at the moment. If they were seen by the soldiers guarding the labs then, at least they would not be shouting to the world, "We're enemy agents!" But they were still likely to be searched, and when the guards found their weapons, they'd be in the same boat as if they'd gone full-blacksuit.

So Bolan had decided upon a plan that would have seemed insanity to many top agents around the world.

They would go in the front door as if they owned the Traditional Pharmacy Research Center.

This would, of course, require some special preparation.

But Bolan would get to that soon, after he'd talked further with Hasan.

Soon after Mohammed made the final turn, the overhead streetlights faded behind them and they came to a dead end. Ahead of them was a large construction site. When they had arrived here earlier in the day, Bolan had noted that the dirt work and foundations had already been completed, and two-by-fours, one-by-tens and other pieces of lumber were in the process of going up in what was obviously a new complex of apartment buildings.

Bolan squinted through the darkness. Earlier, the frame carpenters had been putting up the wood that would eventually be insulated and covered with Gyp-Lap, before brick or whatever other outside wall material was chosen. But before Bolan and his entourage had left the site, the framers had begun shutting things down for the day, rolling up the electrical cords to their nail guns, sliding hammers back home into the loops on the sides of their work pants, and performing other tasks in preparation for their departure for the night.

Mohammed pulled to a halt at the dead end.

Bolan kept hold of the hair plugs left on top of Hasan's head, but said, "If I let go, do you think you can behave yourself?"

The Persian nodded as best he could. It was obvious he was trying to keep as many of the plugs in place as possible.

Bolan let go of the man's stubs. But a multitude of short, nappy hairs came out between his fingers. He wiped his hand on the back of the seat, then said, "Ajib, you know where the smallpox and weaponized anthrax cultures are, don't you." The words were spoken as a statement rather than a question. But just as Bolan had expected, Hasan answered in the negative.

"I know nothing about any such thing."

Bolan took in a deep breath and let it out slowly. "You

know, Ajib," he said in a disgusted tone, "I can't tell you how tired I get having guys like you lie to me and try to play games." He waited a second, then went on. "We've got a busy night ahead of us and I just flat don't have time to play twenty questions. Let me see your hand."

"What?" Hasan asked, his expression one of confusion.

"I said let me see your hand," Bolan said. "Are you right- or left-handed?"

"Right-handed."

"Let's start with your left, then."

Hasan extended his left arm over the seat for what he must have guessed was an inspection.

It wasn't. Bolan grasped the man's wrist, brought the Desert Eagle slightly over his head, then slammed the barrel down onto the back of the man's hand.

Everyone in the Highlander heard several of the delicate bones there snap.

Hasan let out a howl even louder than he had before.

"Shut up," Bolan said again. "You give our position away and you'll die immediately."

His words had their desired effect, and Hasan's scream descended to a mere whimpering.

"I don't *like* doing things like that," Bolan said, still grasping the man by the wrist. "But you've been responsible either directly or indirectly for the deaths of who knows how many innocent people. Women and children included. So I doubt I'll lose much sleep over what I just did. And I doubt that I'll lose sleep over doing the same to your right hand in a few seconds, either. If you still aren't cooperating after that, I'll move on to your feet. And after that…who knows."

Hasan had pushed his face as far as he could into his shoulder. The whimpering continued, but in between the pathetic moans he was able to spit out, "I will…cooperate. Just…tell me…what you want me to do."

"Very good," Bolan said. "Okay, I'll tell you exactly what you're going to do." He finally let go of the man's wrist and Hasan immediately grasped his left hand with his right. "You're going to walk us right past the guards at the Traditional Pharmacy Research Center, then into whatever lab the smallpox and anthrax are stored."

"But how can I do that?" Hasan moaned. "They will never let us in."

"By the time we go in," Bolan said, "we'll all have appropriate credentials as scientists."

Hasan shook his head. "The soldiers will not believe you," he said, his voice calming somewhat. "With the exception of Ali and *him*—" he raised his clasped hands to indicate Ahmad, who sat between Bolan and O'Melton "—none of you even remotely resemble Iranians."

"We don't plan to even try to," Bolan said. "This guy—" he extended an elbow slightly toward Father O'Melton "—and I will be posing as Russian scientific consultants. He speaks Farsi. I don't. But being Russian explains that away quite nicely."

"Where are you going to get documentation like that?" Hasan asked.

"Good question," Bolan said. "And the answer is I don't know yet."

As the occupants of the Highlander fell silent, Bolan pulled his satellite phone from his pocket and tapped in the number to Stony Man Farm. After the usual "bounce around" to assist in keeping the line secured, he heard Price say, "Hello, Striker."

Bolan held the phone tightly against his ear on the off chance that Hasan—or any of the other men, for that matter—might pick up on something from the other end of the conversation. Stony Man Farm was the best kept secret in the world. They didn't even share their business with allies, let alone enemies.

"I'm in Tehran," Bolan said into the mouthpiece. "And I need some falsified documents *pronto.* Alert the Bear, and ask him to check his files for the nearest "paperboy" we can trust."

"Hang on a moment," Price said.

There was a click, then Aaron "the Bear" Kurtzman came on the line. "Barb says you need a paperboy?" the wheelchair-bound computer expert said.

"And I need him *fast,*" Bolan said.

"Give me a second…." In the background Bolan could hear the man typing on his keyboard. A moment later, Kurtzman said, "There's a guy right there in Tehran that Phoenix Force used a couple of years ago. It sounds like the same situation as Ali—this guy has done jobs for the CIA." The man in the wheelchair paused a moment. "I'm remembering it now," he said. "Yeah. That's right." Another pause. "Phoenix Force needed quick creds and I hacked into the CIA and located this guy."

"What's his name?" Bolan asked.

"Don't know his real name," Kurtzman said. "He just goes by Kutbah. It means sermon."

"Sermon?" Bolan said.

"Yeah," Kurtzman replied. "The sermon that comes after the Islamic hours of prayer."

Bolan became silent for a moment. Finally, he said, "Just how dedicated to sermons and hours of prayer and Islam in general is this guy, Bear? I don't want him tipping our hand before we even use the credentials he makes for us."

"Can't answer that one, big guy. But he didn't have any trouble working with Phoenix Force."

"Okay," Bolan said. "Just one more 'unknown' aspect in a mission full of them." He glanced from Hasan to Mohammed and finally to Ahmad, realizing that the men in the car who he couldn't completely trust far outnumbered the ones he could. And he was about to add yet another to the list. Then, into the phone, he said, "Give me his location, Bear."

Kurtzman complied.

"We'll head that way," Bolan said. "Do you have a phone number for him?"

"Give me a second," Kurtzman said, and a second was all it took. "Yeah. Got one. Don't know if it's still good, though."

"Well, try to give him a call while we're en route," Bolan said. "If you can get him, remind him of the Phoenix Force deal and tell him we're on our way." He gripped the satellite phone harder with his fist. "And see what kind of reading you get from him. I don't want to walk blindly into the lion's den."

"You got it, big guy," Kurtzman said. "I'll call you back."

Both men pressed their respective buttons to end the call.

And Bolan began giving Mohammed directions to where they were supposed to find the paperboy who went by the name of Kutbah.

10

The process at the paperboy's lair went far smoother than Bolan had expected it to. Even though the man calling himself Kutbah spoke extremely broken English.

"Your man...Bear-man...he call me," he said in greeting, instead of "Salaam" or "Hello."

Bolan looked him up and down as he stood in the doorway. The man wore tortoiseshell eyeglasses, a stained white shirt and frayed brown slacks that looked as if they'd once been part of a suit. When Kutbah smiled, Bolan saw that he was missing several front teeth. And a few more had turned a sickly greenish-brown and looked as if they'd be falling out soon, too.

Bolan and his entourage had just descended the steps to Kutbah's subterranean space beneath a wrestling gymnasium on the ground level. They had driven past the Iranian Ethnological Museum and Gulistan Palace to get there, then found themselves having to park the Highlander several blocks away and stroll through a pedestrians-only bazaar area. The colorful market sold everything from cones of sugar—some of which extended over two feet in the air—to donkey and camel bridles, saddles and saddlebags. The merchants kept up a constant patter as the men passed.

Hasan kept his broken hand in his pocket as he'd been ordered. But the grimace on his face betrayed the pain he was feeling. Bolan wasn't concerned. A few broken bones in the back of the man's hand was nothing compared to the slaughter of innocents for which his al Qaeda friends had been responsible.

Many curio shops met their eyes as they walked. The smells of roasted lamb and other meats filled their olfactory glands. But Bolan had not come to shop or eat.

He had come to change into another person.

"You come in," Kutbah said, standing back and holding the door as Ahmad, O'Melton, Mohammed and Hasan entered the underground den. Bolan was the last to leave the stairwell, and the smell of printer's ink immediately hit his nostrils as he entered the dimly lit room.

Kutbah must have seen one of the men react to the strong smell because he laughed softly. "You not worry," he said when they were all inside. "No print much anymore. Most done with computer these days."

"Fine," Bolan said. "Just so long as it gets done. And done well."

"Get done pretty good," Kutbah said as he turned and led them deeper into his underground operation. "Bear-man, he tell me you need it fast. Like last time with other men— Bear-man's friends. Make fast means make pretty good, not perfect."

"Just how good is 'pretty good'?" Bolan demanded as he followed, speaking to the back of the man's head. "They have to be good enough to fool—"

"They be good enough to fool anybody not testing them in laboratory," Kutbah said as they entered a back room that looked more like a Best Buy electronics store than a print shop. The number of computers scattered around almost rivaled Kurtzman's computer setup back at Stony Man Farm. "They look real to naked eye," Kutbah went on. "Just tiny differences if lab tests run."

By this point the printer had turned around and was facing them, smiling, showing off both the dying brown teeth and the black spaces where the already-dead had once lived. "You take seats over there," he said, pointing to a row of straight-backed wooden chairs against a wall. "First thing, pictures."

As Bolan and the rest of the men dropped into their chairs, the Iranian paperboy moved to a camera mounted on a stand on the other side of the room. Bolan saw another wooden chair directly across from it.

The setup looked no different from an American state tag agency where motorists went to obtain or renew their driver's licenses.

When Kutbah had the camera up and running, he looked back at the men and said, "Okay. One at a time, please."

Bolan stood up, moving toward the chair in front of the camera.

Kutbah snapped several pictures, then said, "Need clothes change."

"What for?" O'Melton asked from the other side of the room.

Kutbah had already walked to a large wooden chest against the wall. Digging through it, he came up with a variety of jackets, a few shirts and several neckties. Then, turning back to O'Melton, he said, "Because you not get all IDs at same time, on same day. You wear same clothes every day?" He tapped two fingers against the side of his head, indicating that O'Melton might want to think a little deeper on this, and perhaps other subjects.

Bolan switched jackets for a few more pictures. Then he added a tie to his costume for even more. When Kutbah had finished, the Executioner had five different "looks" for the forged documents he would need.

Father O'Melton went next. Then Ahmad and Mohammed. Hasan already had his own Tehran University staff card and other ID.

"Now," Kutbah said. "You want what?"

Bolan stood up from the chair he'd slipped into as he waited for the other men's pictures to be taken. "He and I are going to be Russians," he said, hooking a thumb at O'Melton. "We'll need driver's licenses, passports and identification cards as members of the Russian Academy of Science."

Kutbah looked at them doubtfully. "You are sure?" he said.

"We're sure," Bolan said.

"You speak Russian?" Kutbah's voice was skeptical.

"He doesn't," Bolan said. "But I do."

Kutbah shrugged. "If you say," he said. "How about other men?" His eyes went to Mohammed and then Ahmad.

"Make them Iranian," Bolan said. "This man—" he pointed to Mohammed "—really is Iranian." The Executioner had been careful not to use any of their real names since they'd arrived. "All he needs is a phony ID for the university medical school." He paused a second, thinking. "Make him a doctor," he finally said.

"And him?" It was Kutbah's turn to point, and his index finger aimed at Ahmad.

"I must be Iranian, too," the former Hezbollah man said.

Kutbah looked skeptical again. "You speak Farsi?"

"I do." Ahmad rattled off a few sentences that Bolan couldn't understand.

Kutbah shook his head. "Your accent is Arabic," he said.

"My story will be that I come from Abadan," Ahmad said. "On the Iraqi border. The speech of people from border areas is often influenced by the neighboring countries."

Kutbah shrugged again. Then he said, "Someone once told me an American saying."

"What's that?" Bolan asked.

"They said 'The customer is always right.'"

"Words to live by," Bolan said.

"Gentlemen, then please take seats again," Kutbah said. "This not take long."

Bolan and the others returned to the wooden chairs against the wall and waited as Kutbah went to work on his computers. Every so often a printer would cough into life and a document would come sliding out into the tray. As soon as it had, Kutbah would go to work with a large pair of scissors, cutting the ID card out before reaching for a huge roll of lamination plastic.

Each ID was then stacked on the desk between computers.

Bolan looked at his watch. It was nearing 11:00 p.m., and it would be the early morning hours before they returned to the university campus. All evening classes would have been over for a long while by that point and it was an extremely unlikely time to visit *any* of the buildings, let alone a special one that housed smallpox and anthrax cultures. Just having a university professor—one not even from the medical school—along to break the ice with the soldiers guarding the place wasn't likely to be enough.

In his mind's eye, Bolan could picture an Iranian soldier calling in on his walkie-talkie to verify whether or not such nocturnal visitors had been authorized to enter the building or not.

And that would lead to disaster.

No, Bolan thought as he continued to wait. They needed something more. Some familiar face that the guards would recognize and trust. Someone with the "pull" to make the soldiers think twice about causing him any trouble.

They needed someone directly from the Tehran University of Medical Sciences.

Hasan was sitting next to Bolan as the computers and printers continued to whir, squeak, cough and belch. Bolan knew that the man must know someone with influence at the medical school. But if he asked if he had such a contact, Hasan could simply say no. And Bolan didn't have time to break his other hand and extract the information he needed in that manner.

So he decided to try another tack. One that he hoped would make Hasan believe he knew more about the professor and the university than he actually did.

Leaning to his side, Bolan whispered in a low voice that Kutbah, busy on the other side of the computer room, wouldn't hear. "I can't remember the name of your friend at the Traditional Pharmacy Research Center."

Watching Hasan out of the corner of his eye, Bolan could still see the pain brought on by the broken hand in his jacket pocket. The man had had trouble getting it in and out of his sleeves during costume changes for the photos, but Kutbah either hadn't noticed or didn't care. Bolan saw the Persian professor's face suddenly reveal a mixture of surprise and fear. When he said, "I have no such friend," they were the least convincing five words the soldier had ever heard. So he decided to push harder.

"You don't think we checked you out before deciding to use you?" he said. "Get real. Your friend's name has slipped my mind momentarily, but all I have to do is refer to my notes when we get in the car." He waited a second to see if his bluff was working.

Hasan licked his lips nervously.

It appeared that it was.

But the confused man remained silent, so Bolan added, "Of course, if I have to go to my notes, I'm going to feel like you don't want to help me. And that's going to really hurt my feelings." His tone of voice had a slightly sarcastic ring to it. "So, if I have to do that, I'm going to break your right hand like I did your left."

And that was all it took.

"Ibraham Dunyazad," Hasan blurted out. "Dr. Ibraham Dunyazad. He is the director of the TPRC—the Traditional Pharmacy Research Center."

"That's right," Bolan said, nodding. "Just slipped my mind for a moment." He glanced at the chronograph on his wrist once more. "I've decided we're going to need a stronger tie-in to the TPRC. Someone with clout."

Hasan looked perplexed. "What is this thing you mean?" he said. "Someone with clouds?"

"Clout," Bolan said. "Influence." When he saw Hasan's frown relax, he went on. "If we try to get by the soldiers with just you—a professor who isn't even with the medical school—they're going to have to check and double-check us, and we can't pass muster if that happens. So I want you to give the good doctor a call." He pulled his phone out of his sport coat and handed it to him.

The professor looked down at it as if it might be a cobra sticking its head out of a basket to the music of a flute. Then he looked at his own watch. "Now?" he said. "It is almost eleven-thirty. He will be sound asleep."

"Then you wake him up," Bolan said. "Tell him there are some Russian experts just in town for the night and they need to meet with him at the research center. Tonight. Immediately."

"He will not come," Hasan said, shaking his head violently.

"Yes, he will," Bolan said. "Don't tell me your country hasn't been supplied with all kinds of arms and technology from Russia—I know better. It's not only a secret that's slipped out, it's common knowledge all over the free world." He drew in a breath, still watching Hasan's face. "You tell Dr. Dunyazad that these Russians need to see him, and they've got something interesting for him but don't want to talk about it over the phone. He'll come."

"But what if he doesn't?" Hasan asked.

"Then I'll have to assume you didn't do your best," Bolan said softly. "That you held something back, or said something to alert him that all of this wasn't on the up-and-up. And if that happens, I'll have to kill you." He glanced meaningfully at the phone. "So I'd suggest you be convincing."

Father O'Melton, on the other side of Hasan, had been listening to the entire conversation. He leaned toward the professor and said, "Look on the bright side, Ajib. If he has to kill you, at least your hand won't hurt anymore."

Hasan looked up at O'Melton. Then to Bolan. Then back to the phone.

And then he began to tap numbers into the instrument.

DR. IBRAHAM DUNYAZAD SOUNDED wide awake when he answered the phone a few seconds later, Father O'Melton thought. Bolan had put the satellite phone on speaker, but turned the volume down so the man who called himself Kutbah—on the other side of the room, still working on their false documents—couldn't hear.

Not that O'Melton really thought Kutbah was a security danger. The funny little Persian had as much to lose as they did if anything got reported to the Iranian police or military. But if the priest had learned one thing about the big American, it was that he took no unnecessary chances. He took risks, of course. There were always risks involved in clandestine warfare; O'Melton had learned that in the U.S. Army Rangers. But Bolan always made sure they were carefully calculated.

In many ways, Father O'Melton felt as if he was back in his old Ranger unit, which had often worked hand in hand with the CIA, NSA and other American intelligence groups. The only difference was that this time his unit's leader was in a league of his own. The priest had never seen a man so strong, fast or smart. And he was one of the few soldiers O'Melton truly knew he would follow into hell and back.

As the conversation between Dr. Dunyazad and Hasan began, the irony of this thought struck O'Melton and caused a grin to spread across his face. *To hell and back,* he thought again. That overused cliché took on new and added meaning when it came from a priest.

Bolan had put him in charge of monitoring the conversation, since the big man didn't speak Farsi—about the only shortcoming he had that O'Melton could see. And all it served to prove was that he was human rather than Superman. He spoke fluent Russian and other languages, the priest knew. But he couldn't be expected to know every tongue on the face of the earth.

Which sort of made O'Melton feel special. There was no doubt who was in charge of this mission, but the priest's knowledge of Farsi made him feel he was at least contributing something invaluable to the operation.

Of course Mohammed and Ahmad spoke the Iranian language, too. But O'Melton knew that Bolan didn't fully trust either of them.

The dialogue between the two men began with Hasan relating the same story about visiting Russian scientists that Bolan had told him to tell. And, as expected, Dunyazad tried to change the meeting to the next morning. He even offered to come in early if the utmost secrecy was required. But Hasan stuck to his guns, swearing up and down that the meeting at the research center had to take place this night. Immediately. Eventually, the man on the other end of the line gave in and promised to meet them on campus in an hour.

Father O'Melton breathed a sigh of relief when the call ended, then he glanced at Bolan and gave him a thumbs-up to indicate that it had gone as planned, and there did not appear to have been any hidden messages in the conversation.

On his other side, he heard a swooshing sound, and turned to see that Ahmad had crossed his legs on the chair where he sat. There was a small frown on his new convert's face, and he realized that Ahmad had been listening to the phone call, as well.

O'Melton nodded at the man. Ahmad smiled and nodded back.

Their area of the room fell into silence now, and the only sounds came from the other side as Kutbah finished up their new IDs. O'Melton looked straight ahead, but watched Ahmad out of the corner of his eye. Every fiber in his being wanted to believe that the former Hezbollah man's conversion to Christianity was sincere rather than a ploy to get inside a mission such as this and sabotage it. Father O'Melton was a priest, after all. He believed in Jesus Christ as the Son of God, and evangelism was a big part of his duties. But O'Melton had lived a very different kind of life during his first thirty-odd years—the life of a high school football playing girl-chaser, then a college student involved in martial arts—and girl-chasing. And finally an Army Ranger. Who continued to like the ladies. His was a worldly past before salvation and the calling to priesthood, and that past experience kept him from being naive in his approach to both Christianity and life in general.

God was truly incredible, Father O'Melton knew from firsthand experience. He could take a man's sins, forgive them, then even use them for his own purposes inside his master plan.

O'Melton looked toward Ahmad again. The priest had read the Koran, and knew that Mohammed sanctioned Muslims masquerading as Christians or Jews if it furthered the purpose of jihad. It was an obvious advantage over O'Melton's Christianity, in which denying your faith was a cardinal sin. And this advantage had often made the priest wonder if Mohammed had not sat down one day with the writings of both Jews and Christians and said to himself, "How can I defeat them both?" Then had come up with his doctrine.

Still using his peripheral vision, O'Melton eyed Ahmad further. Could this man be faking it? Could he just be pretending to accept Christ as his personal savior, while waiting for the right time to see that Bolan and he were killed? Could Zaid have some big plan they were unaware of, in which he would self-destruct, too, then wake up in Paradise?

Across the room, Kutbah finally rose to his feet, gathered up all the documents he had produced, and turned toward the group. He crossed the concrete floor, then handed the stack to Bolan, who began distributing the various passports, professional identification cards, driver's licenses and other IDs to the appropriate individual.

When every man had his own set of falsified documents, Bolan turned back to the Iranian "paperboy." "How much do I owe you?" he asked, reaching into his pocket.

Kutbah waved a hand in front of his face. "Already taken care of by your Bear-man," he said. "My money already transferred to account for me. I just check."

"You gave him your account number?" The big American asked. Doing so meant taking a chance not only of getting stiffed on the job, but getting caught, as well.

"I not have to give him," Kutbah said. "He already have, somehow." He shook his head in dismay, but also with obvious respect for the "Bear-man's" professionalism and mastery of hacking into any computer files to which he wanted access. He finished by saying, "Bear-man honest with me last time. He be honest again, I know this thing."

Bolan looked at the other men as they rose from their chairs. "Then we're off," he said. "And we thank you, Kutbah."

"Pleasure in this thing is being mine," Kutbah said in his

broken English. "Now, I finish with words I learn from man who was here last time Bear-man hire me."

"And what are those words?" he asked.

"Y'all come back now, y'heah?" Kutbah said in his thick Persian accent.

O'Melton saw a smile come over Bolan's face. He must have known which man would have been from the South, and used such words.

Without further ado, their leader turned and led the way back up the steps to the street. Father O'Melton was right at his heels, and the other men behind him. He glanced at his watch when they reached the sidewalk and saw that it was almost one in the morning. Approximately fifteen minutes had elapsed since Dr. Dunyazad had promised to meet them at the Traditional Pharmacy Research Center, which meant they had forty-five minutes to get back to the campus.

"Is everybody ready?" Bolan asked as they huddled around him in the cool breeze of the early morning.

All the other men's heads nodded.

"Make sure no weapons are showing," the big man cautioned.

A few minor adjustments were made.

"Okay then," Cooper said, "let's go see how well these fake IDs hold up."

"What have we got to lose?" O'Melton said offhandedly.

"Our heads," Ahmad said immediately.

The big man leading the mission just nodded as he started toward the Highlander.

11

Bolan and his steadily increasing entourage arrived back at the medical school campus thirty minutes later, getting them to their meeting with Dr. Dunyazad precisely on time. The same parking lot where they'd been before was nearly deserted at this hour. The only vehicles still there were two Iranian military jeeps and a Buick LeSabre, which Bolan assumed must belong to the doctor himself.

As he pulled up on the other side of the Buick, Bolan saw that he must be correct. A short, paunchy man with gray hair on the sides of his head and a bald pate stood in front of the Traditional Pharmacy Research Center building, illuminated by an overhead light.

"That him?" Bolan asked.

"Yes," Hasan said. "That is Dr. Dunyazad."

Bolan let the professor lead the way from the parking lot pavement up onto a grassy area, toward the sidewalk to the center. But as he followed, Bolan saw two dark forms approaching from the opposite direction. Dunyazad must have heard their footfalls, too, because he turned around.

As the figures drew closer to the lights on the front of the building, Bolan was able to make out more details. Both were dark, swarthy men wearing OD green BDUs and caps with Iranian military markings. And both carried AK-47s on slings hung from their shoulders.

The rifles were pointed outward, in the assault position, rather than resting across their backs.

The distinction and implication were not lost on Bolan.

While they were still beyond hearing distance, Hasan suddenly twisted his head and spoke over his shoulder. "This will never work," he whispered. "The soldiers will find out we are not here legitimately."

Bolan didn't want the men approaching from Dunyazad's rear to see the profile of a weapon in his hand. And the Beretta, and especially the Desert Eagle, were far too large to draw and keep hidden. But he needed to make a point with Hasan, he had to make it fast, and it needed to be dramatic enough to make the man more afraid of him than the soldiers.

So Bolan reached into his pocket and pulled out the North American Arms .22 Magnum Pug, keeping it hidden in his palm as he took a quick step forward to catch up with Hasan. Then, extending his arm behind the man's neck, he cocked the hammer.

Hasan recognized the sound immediately and a small gasp came from between his lips. "What the soldiers will find is one dead professor if you don't pull this off and do it well," Bolan whispered.

The professor nodded quickly, then gulped, the knot in his throat looking as big as a tennis ball as he swallowed. A moment later, the Pug was uncocked and back in the Executioner's pocket. And Bolan was reminded of how brave al Qaeda members and sympathizers were when in groups, or when attacking the helpless. But just like Hasan, they were cowards with a capital C when the odds weren't stacked phenomenally in their favor. At least that had been the Executioner's experience.

He and Hasan stepped up onto the concrete entryway in front of the building at the same time the soldiers did from the other direction. Hasan greeted Dr. Dunyazad, then turned to the soldiers and spoke in Farsi. The two men frowned, then one of them, with curly hair jutting out from the sides of his BDU cap, replied with a hint of anger in his tone.

Bolan had no idea what they were saying, but a glance at O'Melton told him everything was not going perfectly.

He didn't like not knowing what was going on. Particularly during a time as tense as this. So, taking a step closer to Dunyazad and the men with the AK-47s, he said in Russian, "Do either of you two speak my language?"

The shorter of the two military guards looked up. "I speak Russian," he said in that tongue.

"Good," Bolan said. "Has the good doctor explained to you why we are here?"

"He has told us you are to perform some kind of inspection," the soldier said.

"That is correct," Bolan said in Russian. "So, is there a problem?"

"A big problem," the shorter man said. "We were not informed that there was to be anyone entering this building tonight."

Bolan didn't miss a beat. "That's because this was to be a surprise inspection," he said.

"What are you planning to inspect?" the short soldier asked, as his partner, who obviously spoke no Russian, looked on dumbly.

"That information is above both your pay grade and security level," Bolan said. "But I can tell you this—part of our report will be about the security around the building. Meaning *you*." He let the information sink in, then went on. "And if you do not ask for our credentials, and ask for them quickly, I am afraid I will not be able to give a good report in that regard."

The soldier's brown face turned gray under the lighting. "I was just about to do that very thing," he lied.

Bolan reached into his coat pocket and pulled out one of the well-worn wallets that Kutbah had provided for them to carry their phony credentials in. Spreading the various IDs out like a hand of cards, he picked out the one that named him as a member in good standing of the Russian Academy of Science, and handed it over to the man with whom he'd been speaking.

The Iranian looked at the picture, then Bolan's face, then back down to the card again. His lips moved slightly as he read in the foreign language. Then, puffing himself up importantly, he said, "I will need to see such credentials from everyone who enters the building. And a passport from each man."

One by one, they all handed over Kutbah's forged credentials.

The short soldier made a show of inspecting each card, obviously worried that the Russian would report back badly to his supervisor. Finally, after he'd returned the last set of documents, he said, "You may enter the building."

Dr. Dunyazad pulled a large key ring from his pocket, found the appropriate key and inserted it into the lock on the front door of the Traditional Pharmacy Research Center.

"We will accompany you," the Iranian soldier said as the men started into the building.

Bolan turned to him. "No," he said. "You won't."

In this contest of wills, Bolan obviously had the upper hand, and he was reminded of just how easy it often was to gain the psychological advantage if you behaved aggressively and with authority. Even if you didn't actually have that authority.

The Iranians who were guarding this building were no better than frightened, low-level bureaucrats—afraid of their own shadow, and twice as afraid of the harsh punishment their government handed out for mistakes.

The soldier who spoke Russian shrank back visibly, managing to mutter only, "Why? We must—"

Bolan drew in an exaggerated breath of impatience and disgust. "We are professionals, and we do not want you getting in our way," he said. Then, after raising his chronograph dramatically to his eyes, he added, "And we do not have time to argue with you. As I said before, our mission is above your security clearance."

"But—" the soldier said with even less assurance than before.

"That is enough!" Bolan said, halting the man before he could speak further. "Give me the name of your commanding officer. I will take this matter up with him."

The Iranian looked absolutely terrified, and Bolan was thankful that whoever this man's supervisor was, he had to be a holy terror. He could see that in the soldier's eyes.

"Wait for us here at the door if you like," Bolan said. "But if you attempt to enter the building, I will see that you are brought up on charges."

The Iranian had been thoroughly cowed. He nodded, took another step back. His partner, looking totally confused, followed his lead.

"Dr. Dunyazad," Bolan said. "If you please." He indicated the door to the building with a wave of his arm.

Dunyazad obviously spoke Russian as well, and picking carefully through the key ring he held, he chose one and then walked toward the door.

A moment later, it had been unlocked and Dunyazad was holding it open for the rest of the men to pass through.

The ground floor hallway was well lit, and as soon as they were all inside, Bolan indicated that Dunyazad should relock the door. Through the glass, Bolan saw the frightened and confused faces of the two Iranian soldiers. In a final show of who outranked who, he waved his hand, and the two men shrank back into the shadows and out of sight.

"Now," Dr. Dunyazad said. "Perhaps you can tell me why you felt it necessary to call me out in the middle of the night?" The inflection of his voice made the statement a question.

The question had been spoken to Hasan. But Bolan answered for him, still in Russian. "We are here to check the biological agents stored in this building."

Dunyazad's eyebrows lowered. "There are no biological agents here."

Bolan let out a breath as if he was calling upon all his patience. "Dr. Dunyazad," he said, "I have just had to argue with a simple soldier. Do not make me play the same games with you."

Dunyazad just stared at him.

"All right," Bolan said, impatiently again. "Since the small-pox and anthrax were sent here from Iraq, scientists such as myself, from my country, have assisted you in making sure they are kept safe, and ready to use if necessary."

"Then why have I never met you?" the director asked bluntly.

"I do not know," Bolan said. "Perhaps you were away when we did our earlier inspections. But it does not matter. The soldiers have seen our documents. Do we need to show them to you, as well?"

Dunyazad looked lost in thought for a moment. Then he finally said, "No. I suppose you are who you say you are."

"Good," Bolan said. He stared back at the man who had al Qaeda connections, wondering if the doctor was actually a full-fledged member of the terrorist organization or simply a sympathizer. Not that it mattered. As a past President of the United States had said, "Anyone who is not with the U.S. in the war on terror is against us." That Man had served out his terms and there was a new President leading the war, presently. But the policy had not changed. At least not in Bolan's heart and soul.

The rest of the men with Bolan had remained silent ever since the conversation with the Iranian soldier had begun outside. None of them spoke now.

"Take us immediately to where the agents are stored," Bolan said. "The sooner we can make our inspection, the sooner you can return home and go back to bed."

Dunyazad's mouth opened and his lips started to move. But no words came out, and a second later he closed his mouth and turned, leading them to the elevators. Reaching out, he pushed the up button, then stepped back to wait.

Even though it took only seconds, the tension among the men made the elevator's coming seem like an eternity, and the silence on the ground floor of the Traditional Pharmacy Research Center grew even more poignant. When the car finally arrived and the doors swung open, Dunyazad stepped through them without looking behind him.

Bolan and the rest of his group followed.

"The cultures are secured on the seventh floor," Dunyazad said as he pushed the button between six and eight. A moment later they were rising. And a moment after that the doors were opening to reveal a large laboratory.

Bolan followed Dunyazad out, the footsteps of the men on the tile floor the only sound. Dunyazad skirted various tables covered with test tubes and other tools of the scientific trade. At the rear of the lab stood a closed door, and as he walked, the doctor fished through the pocket of his tweed coat again for the large ring of keys.

He found the one he was looking for, inserted it into the lock on the door and opened it. The room they entered next was a storage area, and barely large enough to hold them all. Cardboard boxes containing who knew what were stacked on both sides. But a narrow path between the stacks revealed what looked very much like a bank vault against the far wall.

As soon as he reached the vault, Dr. Dunyazad's hand went to a numerical dial on its face. Then, instead of spinning the dial, he glanced at the other men. "You will please turn your backs," he said.

Bolan nodded, and he and the rest of them faced the narrow pathway they'd just traversed. The irony of the doctor's request didn't escape Bolan.

The clicking sound of the dial spinning back and forth could be heard as the Executioner and his men waited. Old habits were hard to break, and Bolan listened to each turn. The combination consisted of four numbers, alternating right and left, and he guessed that if he had to try to open it himself, he could have come within three clicks of each number just by listening to the length of time it took between each one.

Again, the irony of the situation struck him. After they finished with what they were about, he would have no need to know the combination.

The final bolt opening was more of a clunk than a click, and Dunyazad stepped back and swung the vault door open. He seemed to have finally gotten used to the idea that Russian scientists were assisting his government, as a broad smile covered his face. "Do what you must," he said to them.

The first thing Bolan noticed as he stepped into the vault was that it was climate controlled. On his first look around he counted an even dozen wooden crates on the floor along the perimeter. A variety of test tubes extended from the open tops, sealed with corks and kept from smashing into one another with plastic foam packing worms. On the side of each crate was a label.

Bolan turned to Mohammed and Hasan. In English, he said, "Check the labels. And bring out all the crates containing biological agents." He spoke quickly, hoping that even if

Dunyazad knew some English, he would not be able to follow the words.

That was not the case.

"Why do you need to bring them out of the vault?" the
man in the tweed sport coat asked. "Why can't you check
them where they are?"

"Because that is not the way we do it," Bolan said. He
turned to Ahmad and O'Melton. "You check the labels, too."
In a voice so low it was almost inaudible, he added, "And
check the other *checkers*."

O'Melton and Ahmad nodded in understanding. The man
they knew as Cooper still didn't trust everyone in his group
of followers.

Bolan and Dunyazad stepped back out of the vault to give
the other men room to work. The Executioner watched as the
men squinted at the labels, then picked up crates and hauled
them and their deadly biological contents out of the vault,
through the narrow tunnel between the cardboard boxes and
into the lab proper.

O'Melton set a crate gingerly on the ground near Bolan's
feet. "It looks like all the crates are bios," he said. "They probably put this vault in here for just that reason."

Dunyazad, who still thought the rest of the men were fellow scientists sent to monitor the status of the biological
agents, said, "What exactly is it that you're checking for?"

"To make sure they are safely stored," Bolan said. "And
we'll run a quick test to ensure that they're all weaponized
and ready to use."

"But why carry them out of the vault?" the Iranian doctor asked. "Can't you perform your tests while they're still
inside?" He waved a hand toward the storage room, and the
narrow tunnel through the cardboard boxes.

Intimidation had worked on the soldiers outside the building, and Bolan decided it was time to employ the same tactics

here. "Not that I am required to justify my job to you, Dr. Dunyazad," he said impatiently. "But just this one time, I'll tell you. We're going to have to transport all of these crates to a temporary lab we've set up for the tests."

"There is no need for that," Dunyazad said. His hand went up to his worn tweed coat and brushed invisible lint off the lapel. "I can give you full use of my lab here." Again he waved his hand through the air, this time indicating the room in which they stood.

"You do not have the proper equipment," Bolan said. "And I am tired of explaining it to you."

His words obviously displeased the director, who was used to giving orders rather than following them. And he had been more or less under Bolan's command ever since they had arrived at the TPRC building. Bolan saw the repressed anger on the man's face, and knew instinctively that he was the kind who would do anything necessary to regain control of the situation and restore his self-importance.

Which led directly to a serious tactical error on the administrator's part. In order to restore his own ego and feeling of self-importance, he let slip a detail he should have kept to himself.

"It is good that you are checking them," Dunyazad said, puffing out his chest as if it had been his idea all along. "Because they are about to be used."

Bolan turned to face him. "In what way?"

"It is a most secretive matter," Dunyazad said, a new smirk of arrogance covering his face. "But I suppose you can be trusted. We are about to turn them over to some of our friends."

Bolan nodded. "What friends?"

The question seemed to startle Dunyazad. It jolted him out of his brief moment in the limelight and back to reality. "Why do you ask?" he said.

"Because I want to know," Bolan replied.

"But why do you need to know?" the man in tweed asked.

Bolan shrugged. "I don't *need* to know. I just *want* to know. Call it curiosity." He looked the other man square in the eyes, then allowed a small friendly smile to curl the corners of his mouth. "We are both professionals, doing what we do best. But we seem to have gotten off on the wrong foot." He extended his hand, and Dunyazad grasped it. "To a more friendly, and honest, relationship."

Dunyazad looked Bolan up and down, then obviously decided that if the man had legitimate access to inspect what was stored in the vault, then he had to be trustworthy. "We— my government—are giving them to a local al Qaeda cell. They will distribute them to other cells, and eventually they will be taken to sites throughout western Europe and America."

Bolan had suspected as much. And finally, he had it straight from the horse's mouth. He nodded at Dunyazad. "That's quite an undertaking," he said. "And all I needed to know." Without further ado, he drew the Beretta 93-R and brought it down hard on the side of Dunyazad's head.

The man crumpled to the tile floor of the laboratory before he'd even realized what had happened.

The other men, busily working inside the vault, didn't notice either until they each carried their next crate out into the lab.

Ahmad, O'Melton and Mohammed took the unconscious body in stride. Hasan, however, was obviously concerned and almost frantic as he said, "Why did you kill him?" in a high-pitched, whiny voice.

"Because he's in league with al Qaeda. And I didn't kill him—he's just been knocked out. This way he will not get in *our* way. That's when he would have had to be taken out," the Executioner said. And just to put a bit more fear in the professor, he added, "Maybe I made a mistake. Maybe I should kill him. Like I said, he's working with al Qaeda."

Hasan looked as if he was about to break down and cry. "You do not think I am in league with al Qaeda, do you?" he asked.

"Don't know," Bolan said simply.

Tears welled in the man's eyes. "I will not lie. I know some of them. But I have never helped or worked with them." As one of the tears began to make its way down his cheek, he added, "Please. You must believe me."

Bolan still had the Beretta in his hand. He lifted it and rested the barrel on Hasan's nose. "Give me one good reason why I should believe you," he said.

"Because," the terrified man said, "I know something. I have some other information. Information which you will need to avoid a catastrophe in your country."

Bolan lowered the pistol. "Then I'll let you live a little longer," he said.

All the other men had gathered in the lab, having brought out the twelve crates of smallpox and anthrax cultures.

"We've got to get these out of here safely," Bolan said. "Which means no stacking. Each man carries only one crate at a time." He paused to draw in a breath. "There are five of us. That means we'll need to make three trips."

O'Melton nodded. "What do you expect out of the soldiers we left outside?" he said. "Are they going to snap to the fact that something's wrong when they see us taking all this out of the building?"

"In all honesty I don't know," Bolan said. "I suppose it depends on whether they've been let in on exactly what they've been guarding. On the other hand, the simple fact that they've been ordered to guard this building at all would tell anyone with an IQ a point above a rock that there's something very valuable in here."

"Is there any way to distract them?" O'Melton asked.

"If there is, I don't see it. Anything we do to divert their attention is likely to have the opposite effect and bring even more Iranian soldiers to the scene."

Ahmad, who had remained silent during most of this night-time mission, finally spoke up. "Then we kill them if they try to stop us?"

"If we have to," Bolan said. "But I'd rather avoid an open gun battle if at all possible. Bullets would go through these crates and test tubes like a knife through butter. And I don't have to tell you what that would mean."

All the men nodded gravely.

"We just have to hope for the best," Bolan said.

"And pray for it, too," Father O'Melton added.

"Sure. And pray for it, too," Bolan agreed. "So we may as well get started."

12

Bolan lifted the crate next to where he stood and led the way out of the lab and down the hallway to the elevator. The other men followed, each with his own box of deadly biological agents, packed in plastic foam and carried carefully in his arms. Even Hasan managed a load, despite his injured hand. There was barely room for everyone in the elevator when it arrived, but they were on their way down as soon as Bolan pushed the button and the doors rolled closed.

The entryway was not far off, and Bolan barely had time to spot the two Iranians in BDUs before he was pushing through the glass door. The one who spoke Russian stepped forward. "What are you doing?" he asked in their common tongue.

"We need to run some more advanced tests," Bolan replied as he stepped past the man and started toward the Highlander. "Tests which can't be performed here."

The Russian-speaking soldier frowned. He was obviously getting more suspicious of this situation as time went on.

Bolan kept walking toward their vehicle, half expecting to get a 7.62 mm in the back from the Iranian's AK-47.

But that didn't happen, and a few seconds later he was pushing the backseat down flat to create more storage room for the crates.

The other men had followed with their own test tube filled boxes, looking like a team of ants transporting goods to the ant hill. Bolan watched as he made ready to return to the building for the next load. But he saw a problem as each man took his turn setting a crate in the back of the Highlander.

There not only wasn't going to be enough room for all twelve crates, there wasn't going to be enough for all the men.

As he strode purposely past the Iranian guards on his way back into the building, he saw that the anxiety on the face of the Russian speaker had increased. "Where is Dr. Dunyazad?" he asked.

"Still inside," Bolan said. After all, it was the truth.

As he turned and opened the door, Bolan heard the same voice switch to Farsi. He had no idea what the man said, but a quick glance over his shoulder revealed that the other soldier had walked up next to him.

O'Melton was right on his heels, but Bolan waited until they were inside the building and out of earshot again before murmuring, "Did you catch whatever he said?"

"Huh-uh," the priest said as they walked on toward the elevator once more.

Bolan held the doors back until Ahmad, Mohammed and Hasan were inside, then pushed the button with the number seven on it. As soon as the elevator closed, he said, "Did any of you Farsi speakers hear what the one guard said to the other as we came in?"

They all shook their heads. "They were whispering," Mohammed said. "I could not make out the words."

"Okay," Bolan said. "But we've got a problem. We can't fit the rest of these crates in the Highlander, let alone have room for everybody to ride in it."

"So what do we do?" Mohammed asked anxiously.

Bolan looked to the one-time CIA informant, then eyed the rest of the men in turn. "We're going to have to steal one of their jeeps," he said.

The words caused a sudden silence in the elevator.

Bolan didn't want the men to have enough time to obsess on how dangerous this mission was about to become. So he said, "When we take the next load down, put as many more as you can into the Highlander. Then stack the rest on the ground just to the side of the vehicle. Between our wheels and the jeep next to it. Zaid…"

The former Hezbollah operative looked up at him.

"Zaid," Bolan repeated, "tell the guards in Farsi that we're going to have to make two trips, and we'd like them to keep an eye on the remaining crates after we drive off. That sounds plausible, and I don't want them knowing we're going to steal one of their jeeps until right before we take it."

Ahmad nodded in understanding. "I will do this thing," he said.

The five men returned to the lab and each picked up another crate. They repeated the process of taking them down to the first floor, then carefully stowed them, leaving the last two between the Highlander and the Iranian military jeep.

Bolan watched Ahmad straighten back up and call out to the two soldiers.

As the entourage reentered the TPRC building for the last time, the Executioner hesitated, letting O'Melton catch up to him. "What did he say, Pat?" he whispered.

"Just what you told him to," O'Melton said in an equally hushed voice.

Bolan nodded. He knew that Father O'Melton was no rookie at facing deception, but he also knew the priest desperately wanted Ahmad's conversion to Christianity to be real. Would that desire cloud the judgment of this man of the cloth? Bolan didn't know the answer to that question any more than he knew whether or not Ahmad's change of faith was legitimate.

As Ahmad and Mohammed picked up the final two crates of biological warfare cultures and carried them to the elevator, Bolan and O'Melton dragged Dr. Dunyazad's motionless body back through the narrow passage in the storage room and dropped it onto the floor of the vault. Then Bolan reached up, closed the door and twisted the dial.

So far, so good, he thought. With any luck, they'd be long gone from the scene by the time the director was even found or woke up. Of course that didn't take into consideration that they still had two men armed with AK-47s downstairs who might be growing skeptical of their bluff. Each passing second gave the guards more time to snap to the reality that things weren't quite right.

As he walked back through the storage room from the vault, Bolan adjusted his shoulder rig slightly. Continuing the train of thought he'd been on, he wondered exactly what they would face when they reached the ground floor for the last time. With luck, the two Iranian soldiers would still be standing there, confused. If so, he could draw down on them with the Desert Eagle, disarm them and keep them covered while the rest of the men loaded the extra crates into one of the jeeps. As soon as that was done, and the guards were bound and gagged, their little rescue party could speed off into the night in both vehicles.

But if Lady Luck refused to smile on them, there would be a firefight. A firefight that would be loud and long in the stillness of the nighttime campus, and catch the ears of the rest of the Iranian army soldiers Bolan knew must be stationed around the area. But that was not his primary worry.

The number one thing on the Executioner's mind was that once the shooting started the chance that one or more of the test tubes would shatter and release the bio-agents that were stored inside was extremely high. It was an almost identical situation to the one they'd faced in Syria with the drums of chemical weapons.

But there was nothing he could do about that at this stage.

Another walk to the elevator.

Another trip down the shaft.

Bolan sensed trouble as soon as he reached the glass door to the outside. The only guard still standing there was the one who spoke Russian. His taller partner had disappeared. And Bolan could think of only one reason that might have happened.

The other Iranian guard had gone for reinforcements.

Bolan and O'Melton stepped through the doorway, with Ahmad, Mohammed and Hasan right behind them. The Executioner twisted his head to whisper, "Ajib, you give us away and you'll be the first to die. I promise."

The professor seemed to have developed a nervous tick, and blinked his eyes hard several times. Then he managed to rasp, "Please believe me. I can give you valuable information on other matters." An almost choking sound came from the terrified man's throat. "But I must live to do so."

Bolan filed that last remark in the back of his mind. The Persian was frightened, and might just be hinting at more intel he could provide in order to save his life. On the other hand, the offer might be legit. But regardless, Bolan had more immediate problems he needed to attend to.

When he turned back around, he saw that the Russian-speaking guard had encircled the pistol grip of his AK-47 with the fingers of his right hand. Although he had not yet raised the weapon to aim at them, doing so would require only a split second. "Take these last crates to the stack between the Highlander and jeep," Bolan whispered to Mohammed and Hasan. "I'll handle things here."

Neither of the two spoke, they just did as they'd been told.

O'Melton and Ahmad flanked the big American as he let a broad smile cover his face. He walked closer to the guard. "Where is your partner?" he asked, glancing behind the man and to the sides for any sign of the second Iranian.

Suddenly the guard *did* bring the barrel of the assault rifle up, aligning the hole at the end with Bolan's midsection. "He will be back in a moment." The soldier took time to clear his throat, then added, "There is something very strange about all of this. When I called in to my commanding officer a few minutes ago, he knew nothing about a scheduled inspection—and especially a pickup of anything—for this building tonight."

Bolan shook his head and blew air through his clenched lips in disgust. "Bureaucracy," he all but spit. "They can't get anything straight, can they?"

The soldier didn't answer. Instead, he asked, "Where is Dr. Dunyazad?"

Bolan didn't hesitate. "Still inside," he said. "There was some paperwork to be done concerning all this, and he wanted to get it finished before he went back home for the night."

The soldier with the Kalashnikov didn't look convinced.

Turning briefly toward the parked vehicles, Bolan saw that the men had the last four crates together, right beside the closest jeep. They needed to load them on, and he needed to find the key to the vehicle. And if at all possible, that had to be done before the other guard and his reinforcements returned. But as soon as Bolan's team started filling the jeep, this Russian speaker would plainly see that they were up to something.

That didn't really matter any longer, however. Time had run out.

Bolan nodded toward the Highlander. O'Melton nodded back, then headed toward the four remaining crates.

At the same time, Bolan turned back to the guard. Twisting his body out of the center line of fire, he lunged forward and hooked an elbow under the AK-47, between the stock and magazine. His other hand grasped the barrel, and by pulling down on the front of the weapon, and jabbing up with his elbow, he wrenched the assault weapon out of the man's hands.

Bolan lifted the AK high over his head, slipping the assault-style sling off the soldier's head. Then he spun the weapon around with the practiced grace of a baton twirler, and the Kalashnikov wound up with the pistol grip in his right hand and the fore end in his left. As he tightened his finger on the trigger, he saw a half-dozen men dressed in Iranian BDUs come running toward him, perhaps forty yards behind the Russian speaker.

One of them was the guard's partner.

Bolan instinctively slid his left hand under the rifle, his fingers finding the selector switch. It was still set on Safety, and he pulled it down to full-auto mode.

A 3-round burst thudded point-blank into the Russian-speaking Iranian's chest and the man flew backward as residual blood from the rifle rounds filled the air.

"Get 'em loaded!" Bolan shouted to the men around the vehicles. "And O'Melton! Take the wheel of the Highlander!"

The soldiers running across the campus heard the shots and slowed slightly, trying to get some sense of what was going on before they sprinted into a possible ambush. Bolan turned their way and sent a long full-auto blast in their direction. They were less than thirty yards away now, and five of the six hit the ground or dived behind trees. The sixth man continued racing forward. He was less than ten yards away when Bolan changed from cover fire to aimed fire. And a 6-round burst stitched the man from navel to throat.

He dropped his AK-47 and plunged headfirst into the grass.

The men who had taken cover hesitated a moment, giving Bolan the chance he needed. Quickly frisking the Russian speaker, he found a key ring in the front flap pocket of the man's BDU pants.

The soldier who had been the partner of the man presently on the ground poked his head around a tree in the distance.

Bolan recognized the face immediately. And just as quickly shot it off.

Turning toward the men at the vehicles, the Executioner yelled, "Heads up!" and tossed them the key ring. Ahmad was the closest, and he stabbed a hand into the air and caught it.

"Find the right key and get the jeep started!" Bolan ordered.

A second later, another brave but stupid Iranian bolted from behind the tree where he'd taken cover, and came lumbering forward. He was a heavyset man with a short-cropped beard, and he raced awkwardly toward Bolan, wildly firing his own AK-47 as he ran. None of the 7.62 mm rounds came within twenty feet of their target, and Bolan took his time, squeezing the trigger and hitting the man twice in the chest, then once through the bridge of his nose.

Three down, the Executioner thought.

And three to go.

From the edge of the parking lot, Bolan heard Ahmad call out, "I cannot find the key! None of them fit!"

Bolan knew there could be two explanations. One, they had loaded the last four crates into the jeep that belonged to the other guard—the nearly headless man who had fallen behind the tree in the distance. Which meant *he* had the key to the vehicle they were trying to start. And getting to him for a search would be all but impossible.

The other explanation was more ominous. It was always possible that Ahmad's conversion to Christianity was a sham, as both Bolan and O'Melton had realized all along. If so, this might well be the moment the man had been waiting for. A situation in which he could sabotage their efforts and get them all killed.

Ahmad would die, too, of course. The soldiers would not

be able to distinguish him from the others. But that would matter little to a Hezbollah-trained potential suicide bomber who was ready to give up his life and become a martyr for the "cause."

Another of the new military guards who had been called into action went down behind a tree and began firing from the prone position. His full-auto fire whizzed past Bolan's face far closer than the rounds of the earlier, clumsy man. Bolan fired twice, the first 3-round volley skimming the man's back and sinking into a hamstring muscle. A long, lonely scream of pain sang out in the night.

"Try the other jeep!" Bolan called to Ahmad. "Don't move the crates unless the engine turns over!" Out of the corner of his eye, he saw his men scramble from the vehicle they were already in.

Returning his attention to the man in the prone position, Bolan dropped his own body to the ground and aimed slightly lower. And his next volley of fire struck the man in the face and neck.

That ended the howling.

Only two of the guards remained in the distance, and they seemed in no hurry to come out from behind the thick tree trunks that shielded them from Bolan's fire. So he pulled the trigger back again, sending full-auto bursts into both trees, reinforcing the men's conviction to stay low.

The AK-47 ran dry and the bolt locked open. But Bolan found another fully loaded magazine on the body of the dead guard at his feet, dropped the empty one, and hooked the new box up, around the corner and into the Russian assault rifle. As the magazine clicked home, he heard the jeep's engine roar to life.

"Now transfer the crates!" he called out. He turned to see the men scrambling once more to get the deadly bio-agents into the jeep for which they had the key.

Without breaking any of the test tubes.

Bolan fired more rounds into the trees. There might be only two guards left. But that didn't mean more weren't coming. The gunfire would have been heard all over the campus, and there were surely more Iranian soldiers on their way. If he took off this second, by the time he got to the vehicles they would have been loaded correctly and be ready to roll out. But if he ceased firing for long, the two guards cowering behind the trees might regain their courage and resume their assault.

So far, the men had not fired any of their shots at the vehicles. Which told Bolan they either didn't know what the crates contained, or that they were as worried about letting the anthrax and smallpox loose as Bolan and his own men were. If truth be told, the shattering of one or more test tubes could probably be contained. There was very little wind to spread the poisons, and if the men in the jeep and Highlander got away from them quickly, they weren't likely to be exposed.

But containment would mean leaving the vehicles where they were, so Iranian specialists in hazmat gear could solve the problem. Which in turn meant that Bolan, O'Melton, Ahmad, Mohammed and Hasan would have to attempt their escape on foot. Not any easy feat in the middle of Tehran.

Most of all, however, Bolan knew it would mean leaving the scene without the biological agents and without completing his mission. When the hazmat workers were finished, Iran would *still* be in possession of enough anthrax and smallpox to wreak havoc around the world.

Bolan knew he needed to end this gunfight before more soldiers arrived. But if he left with the two men still hiding behind the trees, and took off toward the jeep and Highlander, he was likely to draw their fire closer to the crates.

So far, Bolan had been shooting from the prone position—using the dead body of the Russian-speaking guard as cover. Suddenly, he rose to his feet, leaped over the body and sprinted forward. He made sure his footsteps were loud as he raced directly toward the last two men behind the trees with the zeal of an ancient Viking berserker. He was only ten yards away when the closest man realized what was happening, and was forced to lean out around the tree.

Bolan timed his shots as his feet hit the ground. And a trio of 7.62 mm rounds found their way into the enemy. The first bullet struck steel on the Iranian's rifle, sent a shower of orange sparks up into the night, then skidded into the man's chest. The second two rounds went straight into the throat, severing his carotid artery or jugular vein or both—and sending a fire hose spray of crimson into the air to join the sparks.

The second man's tree was perhaps five yards farther and to the side. He, too, leaned out and sent a volley of fire toward Bolan. But he was scared and unsteady, a combination of battle drawbacks that resulted in shots every bit as inaccurate as those of the heavyset man who had charged the Executioner earlier.

Bolan stopped behind the tree, waited for the fire to stop, then immediately twisted around the trunk and fired point-blank.

A lone, semiauto slug struck the last guard in the middle of the forehead and drove him backward. A look of surprise and confusion covered what was left of his face before he fell onto his back, then began to flop in his death throes like an overturned turtle. Finally, his arms and legs dropped and he stopped moving.

The campus went silent. But a moment later, far in the distance, Bolan heard the sounds of more running footsteps and excited, if muffled, voices.

It was time to get out of there.

He turned and sprinted back toward the parking lot. As he neared, he saw Ahmad behind the wheel of the Highlander and O'Melton at the helm of the jeep. A moment later Bolan leaped into the air, landing gracefully next to the final four crates of biological weaponry in the rear of the topless jeep.

"What are you waiting for?" he called out, and O'Melton backed the vehicle away from the curb and turned it around. A moment later, with Ahmad in the backseat, they were racing across the empty parking lot to the street, with the Highlander right behind them.

Bolan looked back at Ahmad as the man drove. It seemed that once again the former Hezbollah man had proved true. But the Executioner reminded himself that the mission was not yet over. One of two things, however, were a still a fact.

Either Ahmad was totally committed to helping Bolan.

Or he was waiting for some even better situation in which to insure they all got killed.

13

Not often, but sometimes in a great while, Bolan found that he flat-out got lucky.

The Highlander and the Iranian army jeep, packed full of wooden crates and men, made it out of Tehran under the moonlit sky without further incident, even passing two small convoys of military vehicles entering the city, and a lone Tehran police car parked on the side of the road. Bolan watched carefully out of the corner of his eye each time they encountered a potential threat, and saw that next to him O'Melton was doing the same.

When they had reached the city's outskirts, O'Melton finally turned to Bolan and smiled. "And some people say there is no God who watches over us?"

Bolan just smiled back.

The two vehicles moved on, reversing the route they had taken into Tehran until they reached the spot in the road where Mohammed had first picked them up. The sun was just peeking over the horizon as they pulled off onto the shoulder and parked. "Get these things up through the trees and into the clearing where we landed," Bolan ordered. "Everyone but you, Zaid. You take the jeep as soon as it's unloaded, and find a spot where you can hide it."

Ahmad looked at Bolan with a puzzled expression. "What about the Highlander?" he asked.

"Just lift the hood," Bolan said. "It'll look like it broke down, and nobody'll pay it any attention. But the jeep is obviously army. It needs to be out of sight from the road."

By the time he had finished speaking all the wooden crates had been lifted out of the jeep. Bolan watched as the other men began toting the biological agents up the hill toward the trees, and Ahmad got behind the wheel of the jeep, pulled it across the road and disappeared over a small hill.

Bolan was still keeping a close eye on the Hezbollah-terrorist-turned-Christian, assigning him simple, non-life-threatening tasks and watching to see how he performed them. So far, Ahmad had shown no signs of treachery. And he had performed admirably back at the gunfight with the Iranian soldiers. But still, Bolan knew, there was more than one possible explanation for that. The man *might* be sincere in his conversion. On the other hand, he might just be really good in the art of deception, which he believed would further the Islamic holy war.

Back at the medical school campus, it had taken the team three trips to get the crates from the laboratory into the vehicles. Presently, with Ahmad hiding the jeep and Bolan supervising, the going was slower. It took the three men four trips each to carry the crates up the hill, through the trees and into the clearing. But there had been no sign of pursuit since they'd left the scene of the gunfight, and Bolan used the time to pull out his satellite phone and tap in Grimaldi's number.

Bolan had contacted Stony Man Farm's ace pilot during the drive from Tehran, and put him on alert. Unless Bolan missed his guess, Grimaldi should already be closing in on the area to pick them up.

When Grimaldi answered, Bolan heard the sound of flapping helicopter blades in the background. "Go, Striker," the pilot said.

"We're at the site," Bolan said. "Ten-twenty?"

"I'm five minutes out," Grimaldi reported. "It's not a very big clearing. So it's going to be a tight fit."

"I have no doubt you can pull it off," Bolan stated.

"Me, either." His old friend laughed. "If I do say so myself."

Grimaldi was as good with aircraft as Bolan was at combat, and knew it. But somehow, even comments like his last one never came out sounding as if the man was bragging.

Ahmad appeared at the top of the hill a moment later. He was afoot, jogging, and the jeep was nowhere to be seen. "Get on up to the trees and into the clearing," Bolan said as the man crossed the highway. "I'll be up in a minute."

Ahmad nodded, smiled and kept jogging.

Bolan waited until the man had disappeared before beginning to run himself. He wanted to see exactly what the informant had done with the jeep—whether it had been truly hidden or left out somewhere in plain sight where it could be spotted from the air. As soon as he reached the top of the hill, he got his answer. The vehicle was barely visible below in a ravine, covered almost completely with branches and leaves.

It looked as if the former Hezbollah man had truly tried to hide it from both land and air.

Bolan ran back down the hill, then up the incline on the other side of the road. He slowed to a walk when he reached the trees, then made his way to the clearing where they had parachuted upon their entry to Iran. He had just stepped out onto the grass when the sound of chopper blades above met his ears.

Knowing they would be in the small clearing, Grimaldi had traded in the Learjet for a Blackhawk helicopter like the ones used by the Stony Man Farm blacksuits when they'd removed the chemical weapons from Syria. He was hovering above the opening in the trees and preparing to set down. "Get back," Bolan shouted to the other men. "Into the trees. He's barely got room to land as it is."

All of them stepped backward and took up positions behind tree trunks.

A moment later, the Blackhawk was on the ground and O'Melton, Ahmad, Mohammed and Hasan were loading crates of bio-agents into its hold. When they were all secured, the men scrambled on board. As always, Bolan waited until last, then hauled himself up and inside the Blackhawk. Taking the seat next to Grimaldi, he nodded his head.

Stony Man Farm's *numero uno* flyboy began to carefully lift the chopper back into the air.

Mohammed, sitting between Hasan and O'Melton, was impressed. "Your man knows what he is doing," he said to Bolan over the noise of the whirlybird. "A less skilled pilot would have snapped the blades off hitting the tree branches."

"That's why we hired him," Bolan said simply.

The strange combination of warriors and informants flew in silence for a few minutes. By the time the sun had fully lit the sky, they were over water and heading toward the aircraft carrier. Bolan got up out of his seat and stepped back to where Mohammed sat. "You like his flying so much," he told the former CIA snitch, "take my place and watch."

The man nodded and traded seats with him.

Bolan sat down next to Hasan and made his real reason for the seat change clear. "Okay, Professor," he said. "I believe you were going to give me some information that would make me want to let you live?"

"Yes," Hasan said. "Please understand, I am placing my life in your hands when I tell you what I am about to reveal."

The Executioner smiled and tapped the Desert Eagle on

his hip. "Maybe you haven't fully realized the reality yet," he said. "But your life is *already* in my hands. So let's get on with it."

"Word is out about the chemical weapons in Syria," Hasan said. "And it will soon be common knowledge—at least within the world of clandestine warriors—that you have also now taken possession of the biological agents in Tehran." The man's face was gray with fear, and his bottom lip trembled slightly with every word that came past it. "But did you know there is one last WMD that was shipped out of Iraq before the U.S. invaded?"

"No," Bolan said. "But it makes perfect sense."

"It is perhaps the most dangerous of all," Hasan said. "At least to the people of America."

Bolan felt his fist clench. "Then why don't you quit pussyfooting around and tell me what it is?" he said in a low, menacing voice.

Hasan drew a deep breath. "First, I must have your word that you will never reveal where you obtained this information," he said. His voice was low, too. But frightened rather than frightening.

"You've got it," Bolan said. "And while we're on the subject, let me map out the rest of the deal for you. You give me the information, and if it turns out to be accurate, I'll keep my mouth shut about your part in all this, and see to it that you get back to Tehran with no one the wiser."

Hasan took another deep breath. "It is a medium-size nuclear warhead," he finally said, in a voice so low it was almost inaudible. "But Iraq's dictator had only midrange rockets on which to mount it." The words seemed to take his air away, his chest heaved as he added, "So he shipped the warhead and rocket to Venezuela."

Bolan sat back as he took in the message and all its implications. The president of Venezuela had been a longtime

America hater and foe. And he was just the kind of man who would be crazy enough to launch a midrange nuke from his country into one of the United States' large Southern cities. Doing so would kill thousands, if not millions, of Americans. And it could make ground zero uninhabitable for decades to come, which would throw yet another curve in the country's troubled economy.

"How do you know all this?" Bolan asked. "It doesn't sound like the kind of thing the Iranian president would talk over with a university professor."

Hasan had been nervous before. Now he cast his eyes down at the deck of the Blackhawk in shame. "I have a friend," he said. "A friend who is one of the Iranian president's secretaries. She overheard a conversation between him, the Iraqi dictator, and the Syrian and Venezuelan presidents."

Bolan frowned at the man. This revelation appeared to be the hardest for Hasan to disclose so far. Why? he wondered.

And then it hit him.

"I'm guessing this secretary—you said *she*—is married," Bolan said.

Hasan kept his eyes on the deck as he nodded.

"And I'm guessing you're married, too," Bolan went on.

That got him another shameful nod.

"And correct me if I'm wrong, but you aren't married to each other."

"No," Hasan said in a weak voice.

"Well," Bolan asked, "just how well do you know her?"

"As well as a man can know a woman," Hasan whispered again.

"Okay then, Ajib," Bolan said. "I'm not completely up on sharia law, but am I right if I assume bad things—*very* bad things—are going to happen to her if this affair becomes public knowledge?"

"She would be put to death," Hasan said. "Probably stoned."

"And I'm guessing you don't mean stoned on drugs," Bolan said, nodding. "What about you, Ajib? What would they do to you?"

"It is not as clear," the professor whispered again. "The man is usually not held to be as responsible. It is assumed that the woman used her feminine wiles to trick the man beyond what he was able to resist."

Before Bolan could speak again, he heard a change in the helicopter's droning and looked out of the Blackhawk to see the aircraft carrier below. A moment later, they descended slowly down onto a landing pad.

Bolan opened the chopper door and dropped down, instinctively ducking under the still-rotating blades over his head. In the distance, he saw the captain of the aircraft carrier come striding his way. A moment later, the man saluted him, then stuck out his hand. "Good to see you again," he said.

"Good to be back," Bolan said. "We've got a dozen crates full of smallpox and anthrax cultures on board. Can you make arrangements to have them flown to the States for disposal?"

The captain frowned. "You aren't taking them back with you?" he asked.

"We've got to make a side trip," Bolan said.

"Understood," the skipper said. "I've got a SEAL team on board who can take possession of this stuff and get it home safely."

"Good enough," Bolan said. Then, turning back to the helicopter, he shouted to Grimaldi, who was still behind the controls. "Jack, the captain's making arrangements to have these crates flown back for us. I want to supervise the transfer just to be safe." He paused a moment as his eyes flew from Grimaldi to O'Melton, and then to the other three. "We need to unload all of our equipment and transfer it and these men back to the Learjet again." He paused a moment, then said, "Can you take charge of that?"

"No problem at all," Grimaldi said. "But are we still dragging all these guys along with us?" The pilot's inference was unmistakable.

Bolan studied his team's faces again. It was clear that hell itself wouldn't stop O'Melton from seeing this mission to the end. And Ahmad at least *looked* as if he wanted to go. But it was clear that Mohammed and Hasan both had reservations.

Bolan eyed the ex-CIA informant harder. His native Farsi had been invaluable back in Tehran, but Bolan doubted he'd need Mohammed in the Spanish-speaking country where he was headed. Of course, with the obvious connection between Venezuela and Iran, there was always a chance that someone who spoke Farsi would come in handy. But Father O'Melton's grasp of the language should be enough. And it would mean they could get rid of a deadweight noncombatant.

Bolan turned his gaze to Hasan, who was obviously frightened beyond belief. He definitely no longer needed the biology teacher. But he couldn't afford to just let him go free. At least not until this mission was over and the professor could no longer alert his al Qaeda contact.

"No," Bolan finally told Grimaldi. "It'll just be me, O'Melton and Zaid." Dropping a hand on Hasan's shoulder and feeling the man recoil at his touch, he turned to the captain and said, "We'll leave this man with you, and ask you to put him under arrest. You can take him to Gitmo and lock him up until he dies of old age for all I care."

"More than happy to oblige," the skipper said.

Bolan turned to Mohammed. "This one's a little different," he said. "He'll be staying with you, too, but he has an agreement with us. I'll contact my base and have them send a team to take him off your hands, settle with him and escort him wherever he wants to go."

"I smell money in the air." The captain almost laughed.

"Sometimes bullets work," Bolan said. "Other times money."

"Where are we going now?" Grimaldi asked.

"Venezuela," Bolan said, as he began helping the rest of the men unload the equipment bags from the helicopter.

14

Hasan had already told him that word of the chemical confiscation in Syria had reached Iran. That meant that this "axis of evil" made up of Syria, Iran and Venezuela was still closely connected, and that if news about the seizure of the anthrax and smallpox had not yet hit the desk of the Venezuelan president, it soon would.

Probably while Bolan and his little ragtag group were still in the air over the Atlantic.

Security would be doubled—maybe even tripled—around the site where the nuclear warhead and missile were hidden. And Bolan had no idea where to begin looking for this last deadly legacy from the Iraqi dictator.

Next to him, Grimaldi was whistling softly as he guided the Learjet through a light rainfall over the ocean. Ahmad had taken a seat and buckled himself in behind them. As the raindrops splattered against the glass, Bolan lifted his satellite phone to his ear and tapped in the number to Stony Man Farm.

A few seconds later, Price answered with her usual professional voice. "Hello, Striker."

"I need the Bear," Bolan said.

Another few seconds and he had him.

"What's up now, big guy?" Kurtzman asked.

"We're back in the air and headed toward Venezuela," Bolan replied.

"I figured as much," he said.

Bolan was slightly taken back. Then he recalled just how efficient Kurtzman could be with his "magic machines." "You getting internet chatter back and forth from Iran to Caracas?"

"And encoded emails," Kurtzman said. "Almost more than we can keep up with. From Syria, too." He paused a moment, and when he came back his voice was low and serious. "It'll take time to decode it all. But I'd say they know you're coming."

Bolan grunted. "We aren't likely to have time for you to get all of the specifics," he said. "The Venezuelan president has one of Iraq's old nuclear warheads and it's attached to a midrange missile. Pointed at you know who." He took a deep breath. "And he's crazier than a March hare. He's likely to launch it just out of spite for us retrieving the chemical and biological weapons."

Kurtzman waited, not answering.

"I need you to start checking satellite photos of Venezuela, Bear," Bolan went on. "The nuke isn't like the chemical and biological weapons we've seized so far. It won't have been hidden as much as *protected*. So look for unusual activity around Venezuelan military bases. Especially those in the northern part of the country, closest to the U.S."

"I can pull those up right now," Kurtzman said, and Bolan heard the man's fingers tapping keys.

"I've gone back three days—right before your mission started—to get an idea on what things looked like then," the wheelchair-bound computer expert said. "We'll use that as our control group of sorts. Two days ago…looks about the same. Yesterday…there's a little more traffic going in and out of the Carabobo air base near Valencia. And today…whoa, son! Looks like a brothel having a two-for-one sale." He stopped talking for a moment and Bolan could hear nothing but soft, steady breathing over the line.

"Anything else of interest?" he finally asked.

"Yeah," Kurtzman said. He paused again, then finally said, "I'm flashing these photos on and off the screen so fast it almost looks like a movie. But there's a long convoy of what looks like a combination of military vehicles and limousines originating in Caracas. Let me zoom in a little closer…" His voice trailed off again.

A moment later, he was back on. "It looks to me like the military went to the presidential mansion, picked up the limousines, then began escorting them to the base. They're about halfway there now, according to the last photo."

"That's got to be our site," Bolan said, pressing the phone tighter to his ear. "The Venezuelan president wants to be there when they launch the missile. Get in as tight as you can on the base itself, Bear. Can you spot any signs of a missile silo or launch pad?"

"Give me a second, Striker," Kurtzman said and again all that came over the line was his soft breathing. Then, "Oh, yeah, buddy. There's a silo down there all right. Looks to me like it opens at the top, right before launching. Fact is, it looks a lot like something out of a James Bond movie. Just smaller." The computer man stopped talking for a moment and Bolan could hear clicks. He had to assume Kurtzman was moving the photo around on his screen, taking a look at the silo from every angle he could. After a minute or so, the man in the wheelchair spoke again. "It's a launch silo, all right. And it sticks out like a sore thumb. Set a little ways off from the runways."

"You're *sure* there's a missile hidden under there?" Bolan asked.

"I'm not *sure* of anything," Kurtzman said. "But if the nuke and conveyance system were sent before the U.S. invaded Iraq, they've had plenty of time to build a launch site.

And I can't think of anything else they'd want to hide this far north, can you?"

"No," Bolan said. "I can't. That's got to be our place."

"I agree," the wheelchair-bound man said. "But how do you plan to zip in and get a nuclear warhead and its missile out of there with an entire military airbase surrounding you? You can't load it on the Learjet, and even if you could, they'd shoot you down before you could even get up in the air again to *get* shot down."

Bolan felt his teeth grind together. Kurtzman was right. There was no way he, O'Melton and Ahmad could invade the base and secure the nuke by themselves.

Then a familiar voice suddenly broke in on the line.

Hal Brognola.

"Hello, Striker," the Stony Man Farm director of sensitive operations said. "Hope you don't mind my doing a little eavesdropping."

"Not at all, "Bolan said. "You have any ideas?'

"As a matter of fact, I do," Brognola said. "Hang on. There's someone else I'm going to add to this conference call. He wants to lend a hand if he can."

"It it's who I think it is, he's certainly welcome to come on board," Bolan said. Then he smiled. Because he knew who he was about to speak to. And he also knew that what had been impossible short seconds ago had just become "doable."

Dangerous. But possible.

"HERE'S WHERE WE STAND," the President of the United States said in Bolan's ear. "I'm mobilizing so many fighter jets the Venezuelans will think they're on the set of Alfred Hitchcock's *The Birds*. They're for show, and won't fire or even land unless they have to. But I'm also sending one C-130 filled with Delta Force personnel. Delta's got several men trained in nuclear disarmament, and as soon as the C-130 hits the ground they'll break down the missile and warhead and load everything onto their plane."

Bolan paused a second. "The Venezuelan leader is going to scream to high heaven about the U.S. invading his country," he finally said. "He'll call it an act of war."

"Let him scream all he wants," the President said. "What *he's* doing is an act of war."

"Okay," Bolan said. "But with all due respect, if you've got all of that coming down to get the nuke, what do you need us for?"

"Because while they're always in a state of semireadiness," the President said, "it still takes a little time to get all of these planes mobilized. You're already on your way, and you're much closer." He sucked in a long, stress-filled lungful of air before going on. "I need you to breach the base and take over the control room within the launch silo. You've got to stop the Venezuelans from launching the warhead until we get there and can scare them out of it."

"That's affirmative," Bolan said. "But the base will be on high alert. That means we're going to have to drop in from the sky again, and hope we can land and carry out the mission while being outnumbered at least a hundred to one."

"Do whatever you have to do," he heard the President say. "Just make sure the missile doesn't get off the ground. It's my understanding from Kurtzman that the Venezuelan president is actually going to the base himself?"

"That's what it looks like," Bolan said.

"Then as soon as you've secured the control room, take custody of him if you can, and give me a call. We'll time it so the fighters zoom over the base about that time. We'll treat him to a show of force and see if he can't be reasoned with."

"You've got it," Bolan said. "Talk to you as soon as the control room is secured." He was about to end the call when Kurtzman reentered the conversation.

"I've finally hacked into the Carabobo launch system," he said. "The missile is aimed at Miami."

"That's about the closest major city," the President said. "It makes sense."

"Can you shut the system down, Bear?" Bolan asked.

"Unfortunately no," he said. "There's a code word that has to be typed in at the site. So even if I had the word, it wouldn't do us any good. Any attempt to shut it down incorrectly automatically launches the missile."

"Then we'd better get our chutes on," Bolan said. "We're only a few miles out."

"Good luck," the President said.

Father O'Melton shook his head and laughed softly again. "How many times do I have to tell people?" he asked no one in particular. "Luck has nothing to do with it."

The priest crossed himself and closed his eyes tightly for a few minutes.

Then all three warriors changed into blacksuits.

THEY HAD BEEN FIRED ON by ground troops as soon as the Venezuelan soldiers on the ground inside the base saw them floating down through the air. Miraculously, the only round to come even close to finding its mark had hit Ahmad's backpack. But it had done him no damage.

Bolan's boots hit the ground and he took two quick steps to gain his balance. In his right hand he held an H&K MP-5, fully loaded with a 30-round 9 mm magazine. As the gunfire continued around him and the other two men, he accessed the Spyderco Navaja with his left hand and quickly sliced through the lines connecting him to the nylon canopy that had fallen next to him. As soon as it was free, the parachute began blowing across the grass toward the runways.

At least a hundred men sprinted toward them, AK-47s firing wildly as they ran. In addition to that barrage, several more Venezuelan soldiers guarding the silo and the office building adjacent to it raised their own rifles to kill the invaders.

Bolan pulled the trigger back on the MP-5 and sent a 3-round burst at the men crossing the runway nearest the silo, then turned his attention away from them. They were still too far away to hope for anything more than a lucky shot at the three fast-moving targets, and the silo guards were the bigger threat. So as he sprinted brazenly for them, with O'Melton and Ahmad at his heels, he opened up with a duo of 3-round bursts that took out two of the men in OD green.

From next to him, and just a step behind, Bolan heard the familiar sound of another MP-5 and watched a third guard drop. O'Melton. The man was familiar with the state-of-the-art German submachine gun, and had chosen it from the Learjet armory as his primary weapon, just as Bolan had.

Then a much different sound—a larger caliber rifle—burst from Bolan's other side. Yet another of the silo guards went down, clutching his chest in death. The sound of this weapon was also familiar. An AK-47, just like the Venezuelans were using. But this one was in the hands of Ahmad.

Ahmad's training had been a little different. He had learned his craft from Hezbollah, so the Russian-designed Kalashnikov rifle had been his weapon of choice. Bolan found it slightly ironic that the man was presently using skills the terrorists had taught him for use against the West. So far, Ahmad had proved to be as good as his word about switching sides in the war on terror. But would this be the time when he suddenly showed his true colors and sabotaged Bolan's mission? Would he find a convenient time to shoot Bolan and O'Melton in the back, then let the nuclear missile launch go ahead?

Bolan didn't know. But while all these things flashed through his mind, he took time to notice that only one jeep and one limousine were parked outside the office building built into the silo. Did that mean the Venezuelan President was already inside? With only one jeepful of men to protect him?

Why not? Bolan thought. He was on a highly fortified military base and was likely to feel even safer than he did in his own presidential palace.

Bolan squeezed the trigger of his subgun and another Venezuelan went down for the count. All the guards outside the office area were dead now, and Bolan sprinted on to the glass door leading inside. When he reached it, he stepped aside, his back against the brick wall to the left. O'Melton and Ahmad fell in right behind him. Rather than opening the door and framing himself for a multitude of rounds from within, Bolan aimed the MP-5 at the top of the door and switched the selector to full auto. Systematically, he fired, working his way down the door and taking out every shred and splinter of glass until he reached the push bar that opened it. The door came off its hinges with four quick shots, and then Bolan emptied the rest of the 9 mm magazine into the lower half of the glass.

As he'd expected, return shots came zipping through the gaping hole. But by the time he'd replaced the empty magazine with a full load, the gunfire had slowed. And Bolan moved out from the wall just enough to dive through the opening at an angle.

He hit the ground on his shoulder, rolling up onto one knee and taking in the layout of the room in a brief glance. There were three desks inside the launch office, each with a computer. All were along the same wall, and the men behind them looked frightened. They were technical personnel, the military equivalent of "computer geeks." Their real weapon was the nuke in the silo next to them. But that didn't stop them from going for the pistols holstered on the gun belts wrapped around their waists.

Bolan took the first man out with a single shot to the forehead. O'Melton's MP-5 burped out three 9 mm rounds into the second. And Ahmad's AK-47 fired two 7.62 X 39 mm slugs of steel-jacketed lead into the third.

But another trio of men were on their feet. Instead of green BDUs, they wore navy blue dress uniforms with white braid on the chest and shoulders. Presidential bodyguards. They were trying to get a fix on Bolan with their AK-47s.

The Executioner cut loose with a double-tap of 3-round bursts, each one taking down another of the Kalashnikov-sporting men. Then, as the gunfire died down, he turned his MP-5 toward the last man standing.

A short, stocky figure wearing a tailor-made brown suit with subtle blue pinstripes running through the cloth. The man's thin, carefully tended mustache quivered above his upper lip in terror. His hands were out in front of him, palms facing Bolan, in classic "don't shoot" sign language.

Bolan glanced through the window toward the runways, where Venezuelan soldiers were still sprinting toward them. There was only one way to keep them from overrunning the building and launching the missile that would decimate Miami, Florida.

Bolan dropped his MP-5 on top of the nearest desk and drew the Desert Eagle .44 Magnum. Then, taking two quick strides to the man in the brown suit, he reached up and grabbed a handful of the president's hair, turned him around and stuck the pistol barrel into the back of his head, then marched him toward the opening where the glass door had been.

"Tell them to stop or I'll turn your head into a canoe," Bolan demanded.

"Alto!" the Venezuelan screamed.

The oncoming men stopped in their tracks.

Just then, the sound of jet airplanes sounded in the distance. And a split second later at least three dozen aircraft whizzed over the Venezuelan base, wingtip to wingtip. All heads on the base looked upward, but the planes were gone again so fast that their American markings could barely be made out.

In the distance, Bolan watched as the fighter pilots turned one-eighties in perfect formation, then flashed back over the base even lower than before.

Still holding the .44 to the back of the president's neck, Bolan pulled out his satellite phone and called Stony Man Farm. A moment later, another conference call had been set up with the American president.

Bolan tapped the speakerphone button and held it up where both he and the Venezuelan president could hear.

"President," the American leader said. "You've been up to a little mischief, haven't you?"

"I do not know what you are talking about," the man said, trying to salvage at least some small portion of dignity. "All I know is that your men and aircraft have invaded my country. It is an act of war."

"You *really* want a war with the United States?" the American president asked. "You'd lose, and you'd lose big, and you know it." The President stopped talking. But when he got no reply, he went on. "We'll make this short and sweet. In a few minutes, one of our C-130s is going to land at your base. I have men who'll dismantle your nuclear warhead and the missile with which you planned to blow up Miami, and load all the pieces on board. Then we'll take off. But if you do anything to try to stop us, my jets will be back and blow your little base to kingdom come. Do you understand me?"

"I understand that I will take you to the World Court," the man said. "You will pay billions of dollars in reparations for all of this."

"You do what you have to do on that," the American president almost laughed. "What exactly do you think the court is going to say when we show proof that you had a nuke aimed, armed and ready to blow up Florida?"

Again, he got no answer.

"I'll assume by your silence that we're in agreement," the American said.

"You may assume such," the Venezuelan replied.

"Tell your men to go back to their barracks and wait," Bolan told the Venezuelan president as he ended the call.

The man with the mustache barked out the orders in Spanish.

Bolan dragged him back inside and dropped him into a desk chair that had been vacated when he'd blown a computer expert out of it. "Sit still and keep quiet," he ordered.

A few seconds later, the loud sound of the C-130 transport plane could be heard, and a moment after that the big "bird" landed on the runway nearest the silo.

Roughly two hundred men, all clothed in computer-generated camouflage fatigues, came running out of the plane toward Bolan, O'Melton, Ahmad, the president, and the dead bodies that surrounded them.

The disassembly by the Delta Force nuclear specialists took less than thirty minutes. Loading the pieces onto the plane was even faster.

When the process had been completed, a Delta Force warrior with colonel's bars on his fatigue blouse stuck his head back into the office area. "You and your men need a ride?" he asked.

Bolan nodded. "It sounds better than sticking around here all alone after you're gone," he said.

"Then come on," the colonel said.

Bolan, O'Melton and Ahmad left the Venezuelan president still shaking in fear at the desk, and followed the man out to the C-130. As if to remind the Venezuelan troops one last time to steer clear of the operation, the fighter pilots buzzed the base, less than ten feet above the tallest structures.

Bolan and his men hauled themselves up on board and took seats against the walls of the big transport carrier. The Executioner found himself next to a sergeant, with Ahmad on his other side and O'Melton beside him.

Father O'Melton leaned back against the wall of the plane and closed his eyes once more. Whether it was in weariness or in prayer, thanking God for their safety during the numerous life-or-death encounters they had faced during this mission, Bolan didn't know.

Ahmad turned to Bolan. "I would say we have been successful," the Arab said. "But I am glad it is finally over."

The Executioner just nodded.

The sergeant next to Bolan had heard Ahmad speak. "Couldn't help hearing your accent," he said, as he leaned forward and looked around Bolan. "You American?"

"No," Bolan said, glancing quickly from Ahmad back to the sergeant. "But he's on our side. You can take my word for it."

* * * * *

Don Pendleton
CHOKE POINT

Human trafficking funds a terrorist plot
to overthrow the U.S.

A U.S. senator's murder and the kidnapping of several
children of high-profile government officials leave
the President no choice but to call in Stony Man
to investigate. But the kidnappings are only the tip
of the iceberg of a human trafficking ring. It's a race
against time as Stony Man fights to neutralize
the operation…no matter what!

STONY
MAN®

Available December 2012!

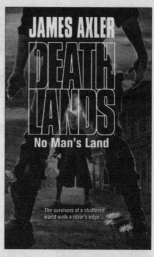